Christmas Wish in a Bottle

by

K. M. Daughters

Copyright Notice

This is a work of fiction. Names, characters, places, and incidents are either the product of the author's imagination or are used fictitiously, and any resemblance to actual persons living or dead, business establishments, events, or locales, is entirely coincidental.

Christmas Wish in a Bottle

COPYRIGHT © 2024 by K. M. Daughters

All rights reserved. No part of this book may be used or reproduced in any manner whatsoever without written permission of the author or The Wild Rose Press, Inc. except in the case of brief quotations embodied in critical articles or reviews.
Contact Information: info@thewildrosepress.com

Cover Art by *Lisa Dawn MacDonald*

The Wild Rose Press, Inc.
PO Box 708
Adams Basin, NY 14410-0708
Visit us at www.thewildrosepress.com

Publishing History
First Edition, 2024
Trade Paperback ISBN 978-1-5092-5937-3
Digital ISBN 978-1-5092-5938-0

Published in the United States of America

Dedication

For Kay and Mickey * Nick and Vi * Tom and
Jeanne * Ed and Edith
Thank you for showing us that bench love is possible.

Acknowledgments

Christmas is our favorite time of year. We sing Christmas carols together sitting under the lit Christmas tree, gawk at houses' Christmas decorations and even walk ourselves frozen in the snow. We start the holiday season every year with a phone call to each other the minute Santa appears in Herald Square at the Macy's Day Parade – let the holidays begin!

Christmas sister-shopping sister forays to check off wish list presents for our families and find sister gifts for each other are cherished memories. We started a tradition years ago when we found an ornament we both loved. After we each paid at the counter, we switched bags – Merry Christmas, Kathie. Merry Christmas, Patti. We liked doing this so much that we extended this practice to shopping in general. We each pay for identical items, switch bags and when asked by interested (nosey) husbands, we can honestly say that the other sister spent her money on the gift.

We hope you, Dear Reader, love Maggie, Kane and Harper's story. FYI all the Outer Banks holiday events featured in the story are true and current. If you're in the area, there's lots of magic to experience.

Thank you to Ally Robertson for your gentle, spot-on guidance in editing our novels. You are so much more than a pro to us. You are a treasured friend and cheerleader. We are ever grateful for you. Thank you to the author-centric Wild Rose Press for making our dream come true since 2008. Thank you Lisa MacDonald for the beautiful cover art. Thank you always and evermore to Joelle Walker, our Fairy God-Editor and adopted sister.

We thank you, Dear Reader, for spending time in the worlds we dream up. We wish holiday blessings to all of you.

Prologue

Outer Banks, North Carolina
January 3, Five Years Ago
Christmas Legend of the Three Butterflies

Kay Layton gazed out at the froth-topped waves pounding the shoreline along the inn's beachfront as she worked at the sink in her kitchen. Her husband, Mike and her daughter, Skye had left to grocery shop after they had finished breakfast to replenish provisions depleted by their seasonal guests. Despite the overcast skies, stormy sea, and now vacant guest rooms after the recent weeks of Christmas cheer, Kay smiled at warm memories. She doubted that she would ever forget the sheer joy on Julie Donovan's face when her son, handsome and resplendent in his Navy uniform, had appeared in the parlor on Christmas day.

Even though magical happenings at her inn were commonplace, Kay hadn't seen the answer to Julie's prayers coming. When the widow had checked in two weeks before Christmas, Kay had only known that Julie's stay on OBX would remove the aura of sadness that seemed to cling to the pretty fifty-year-old.

The holiday season at the Inn of the Three Butterflies was always special, and that year was no exception. Julie Donovan had attended most of the local events and had joined in with the rest of the guests to take part in the full gamut of holiday activities that Kay and Mike had hosted, but it wasn't until her son had surprised her that Julie had come alive with happiness.

Kay wiped the countertop, dried the surfaces with a dishtowel and then hung the towel over the dishwasher's handle. She moseyed out of the kitchen and through the dining room to the front of the inn. Taking a seat at the reception desk that faced the front door, Kay sorted the unopened mail delivered late afternoon the day before. A handwritten envelope with a California return-address captured her attention. She slit the flap with an antique opener, extracted the folded note and read the letter from Julie Donovan.

Dearest Kay,

Since spending Christmas with you I have lived in a state of dream-like wonder. I can scarcely believe that Johnny was with me! The way it all worked out was just short of a miracle. It was the answer to my prayers…or maybe the magical fulfillment of my wish.

The second day of my stay at the Inn of the Three Butterflies, I went shopping in Manteo with a few of your guests. A pretty sea-glass bottle with a cork stopper in one of the shops caught my eye. For some reason I felt I just had to buy that bottle.

I hadn't seen Johnny in over a year since he was stationed in Norfolk. I guess I was spoiled for all the years he was stationed in San Diego nearby. As you know, he's my only child. Since Andy died, time spent with Johnny is even more important to me. Anyway, with Christmas nearing I missed Johnny terribly and found myself wishing with all my heart that we might be together for the holiday.

I wrote that wish on a sheet of the stationery that

you supplied in my room, rolled the paper into a tube, and slipped it inside the bottle. The next day I threw the bottle into the ocean right outside the inn and watched the waves churn it out to sea.

I walked on the beach Christmas morning along the water's edge. Just as I was about to head away from the ocean, a sea-glass bottle with a cork stopper washed up on the sand by my feet. I would have sworn it was the same bottle that I had purchased in Manteo, but it was empty. I scooped up the bottle and brought it to my room.

That afternoon my Johnny walked into your parlor. I don't think it was a coincidence. I think it was magical. Just like your beautiful inn.

Thank you, Kay. I don't know how it was possible, but I believe that my Christmas Wish In A Bottle came true.

Love, Julie

P.S. I'll see you in December. Wouldn't miss it!

Chapter 1

Chicago, Illinois
Five Years Ago

Maggie Larsen awakened abruptly, her heart pounding and tears streaking down her cheeks. The sheets were tangled around her legs, and she had a hard time catching her breath as she struggled to identify her unfamiliar surroundings. She focused on the sterile, white walls as a painful reality dawned. Her sister was gone…forever.

She turned her head to the side on her pillow and gave a start. The deepest blue eyes stared back at her from the bassinet next to the hospital bed. Stacking the pillows behind her, Maggie reached for the tiny baby and cuddled her against her chest.

"My precious little girl."

The baby grasped her finger.

"Are you hungry?"

The newborn latched onto her breast and Maggie leaned back against the pillows while the infant nursed greedily.

Maggie was exhausted but she didn't dare close her eyes. When she did, the nightmare returned.

The journey to giving birth had started on the happiest note. Her sister, Eileen and brother-in-law, Greg, had invited her for pizza and beer at their house.

Eileen had seemed jumpy when she had arrived triggering Maggie to think the worst. Both Eileen and Greg had suffered through aggressive cancer treatments. Eileen had beaten ovarian cancer and Greg had survived prostate cancer.

In addition to their individual medical happily ever after, they had met at a cancer fundraiser and had fallen in love. Eileen believed that the divine purpose of having cancer was to meet the love of her life. Their yearly scans brought angst until they got the great news that the cancer had not come back.

Maggie had prayed that nothing had changed with her sister's health. Her hands had trembled placing the bottle of wine on Eileen's kitchen counter. "Please just tell me. Are you OK? Is Greg?"

"Oh, sweetie, I'm so sorry to make you worry." Eileen had pulled Maggie in for a hug. "We're both fine. Clear scans for both of us."

Maggie had sighed and taken the first unlabored breath since she had entered the apartment. "Then why do you seem so nervous?"

"We have a huge favor to ask of you."

"Anything you need."

"Don't agree to it yet. When Greg gets home with the pizza, we'll talk about it."

"I'm already saying yes."

They had asked Maggie to donate eggs so that they might have the family they desperately wanted. Their plan, if Maggie agreed to be a donor, was to arrange through an agency for a surrogate to carry the baby. Greg's college roommate, Joe, had already agreed to donate sperm. Maggie had not only gone along with the plan, but also had volunteered that night to be their surrogate. She would have done anything for her sister.

The next months had passed in a flurry of anticipation. Maggie had conceived after the first insemination. The trio had celebrated quietly together. After a couple of months of morning sickness Maggie had felt great.

Eileen and Maggie had spent hours shopping and decorating the perfect nursery in her sister's home. Eileen had accompanied Maggie to every OB appointment and had clutched Maggie's hand while tears tracked down their cheeks hearing the baby's heartbeat for the first time. They had shared the baby's first kick. Maggie's due date was December 24th. What an amazing Christmas gift! They had made the sweetest plans.

Greg and Eileen had simply told everyone that they were adopting. No one other than Maggie's parents had known about her and Greg's roommate's roles in the adoption. Maggie had known deep in her heart that the baby was a girl but had never let on to Greg or Eileen since they had wanted to be surprised.

Maggie was a journalist for the popular magazine, *In the Know* and had the luxury of working virtually. When she had attended the occasional meeting, she wore baggy clothes, and never needed to explain her situation. Everything had worked out perfectly until she was a few weeks away from her due date.

Eileen and Greg had decided to take a "babymoon" trip to Hawaii. After a joyful Thanksgiving dinner with Maggie and her parents, Eileen and Greg had departed on the planned two-week vacation. They had sent Maggie daily pictures of sea turtles, glorious sunsets, and beautiful selfies of the pair beaming into the camera lens.

Tears welled in Maggie's eyes as she recalled the

phone call that had turned her blood to ice. She had just sent her latest feature to her magazine's editor and had taken a sip of soothing lemon tea when her phone rang. She hadn't recognized the number. Even so, she had taken the call having a premonition that it was important.

The policeman had informed her that Eileen and Greg were killed in a small airplane crash hopping from one island to another. The impossible news had spurred her to scream and then sink to the floor. Her last memory after that was calling her mother, although she had no idea what she had said to her. And then the stabbing pain in her stomach had blacked out her consciousness.

The next thing she remembered she had awakened in that hospital bed where her mother and father gripped each of her hands. Mom had explained that she had called 911. The paramedics had brought Maggie to the hospital by ambulance and her OB had performed an emergency c-section.

Maggie hadn't regained consciousness for two days. She felt guilty that she hadn't helped her parents deal with the death of their daughter during that time. They had looked exhausted and shrunken when Maggie opened her eyes.

Afterward Maggie went on a roller-coaster ride of warring emotions. One minute she was reeling, missing her sister and the next she was filled with unbridled joy holding the baby.

****

Maggie smiled at the beautiful angel staring back at her. My daughter!

With her beloved sister gone, Maggie was a mother.

The door opened and a sunny-faced nurse who Maggie judged to be in her mid-twenties, poked her head into the room. "You're awake. Wonderful. Good morning, beautiful little ladies. How are you both doing today?" She reached behind Maggie for the blood pressure cuff. "Are you ready to go home?"

"Oh yes!"

Bending near enough for Maggie to inhale her soft perfume, the nurse, whose nametag read, Trudy, expertly took Maggie's blood pressure and pulse. The smile never left Trudy's face as she bent to her task.

She handed Maggie a clipboard explaining the birth certificate and social security forms that Maggie needed to complete.

Trudy scanned both forms after Maggie handed back the clipboard. "You left out the father's name."

Maggie cringed. "I...don't know who her father is."

"No problem. Just write, unknown." She pointed to the blank line without a shred of disapproval or judgment and handed back the forms to Maggie. Maybe Trudy encountered "unknown" fathers of newborns often?

"I'll take your little one to the nursery. The doctor will examine her and if everything is OK, he'll sign your discharge orders. I put the suitcase your mom brought last night in the bathroom. I'll be right back."

A surge of anxiety gripped Maggie as the door shut behind the nurse pushing the bassinet. She hated to let the baby out of her sight. If she had only kept Eileen in her sight, her sister wouldn't be dead.

She swung her legs off the bed, gained her footing and shuffled into the bathroom. Too weary to take a shower, she splashed water on her face and brushed her teeth, looking forward to a nice hot shower later at home. Maggie unpacked a flowing, soft wool dress she had never seen before from the suitcase and slipped it on. The crimson flowers on the black background brought out some color in her cheeks and the material skimmed loosely over her still swollen body. Her sweet mom had thought of everything.

Maggie paced around her bed waiting for the nurse to return with the baby. There was a light knock on her door and then it opened slowly. Her parents bustled into the room loaded down with bags and a giant stuffed pink bear.

"The dress looks lovely on you, darling." Mom gave Maggie a kiss on her cheek and placed all the packages on the bed.

"You're a breath of fresh air, sweetheart." Dad sat the bear in the recliner armchair and then gave Maggie a hug. "I'll be right back. I'll bring up the car seat."

Dad zipped back out into the hallway.

"How are you feeling, sweetie?" Mom perched on the edge of the bed.

"I'm fine. Maybe a little tired. How are you and Dad? You both look exhausted. Is this too much for you?"

"Oh, honey not at all. I think you and our grandchild are all that's keeping us going right now. I hope you don't mind. We moved some of our things into your condo. We thought we would stay a few days and help you out."

"That's perfect. You can stay as long as you like."

"We also spent some time getting the nursery ready. We figured if you didn't like what we did you can always change it."

"I'm sure I'll love it. Thank you. But you're working way too hard."

"We had to finalize the memorial service

yesterday." Mom bowed her head and then took a deep breath, raised her head, and gazed teary-eyed at Maggie. "Setting up the nursery didn't feel like work at all."

Dad returned with the car seat and then took a couple blankets, an outfit, and the cutest snowsuit out of the shopping bags on the bed.

Maggie chuckled. "You're spoiling your granddaughter already."

He winked at her, taking a seat in the recliner holding the bear on his lap. Trudy came into the room with the baby. Dad handed Mom the bear and opened his arms. The nurse gently placed Maggie's daughter in her grandfather's arms.

Grabbing her phone, Maggie took a photo of him gazing at the baby wearing a totally besotted expression on his face.

"Have you decided on her name?" He hadn't taken his eyes off his granddaughter who had wrapped her tiny fingers around his thumb.

"I did…"

She paused. Eileen had never mentioned any baby names that she and Greg leaned toward, and Maggie hadn't pressed for information. She had done everything she could to assure them that the child was completely theirs despite the unusual birth circumstances.

"I've named her Harper Eileen," Maggie said.

"Oh, what a unique name. I love it. It's just perfect." A single tear trailed down Mom's cheek which she hurriedly swiped away with her finger.

She stepped over to the recliner and stood behind Dad smiling down at the baby. "Hello, Harper. We're your nana and grandpa and we're going to spoil you rotten."

"Look, Maggie." Mom flashed her a grin. "Harper is smiling at us."

Maggie captured with her phone camera the baby's fleeting expression which almost looked like a smile.

She dressed Harper, strapped her into the car seat and then an attendant appeared with a wheelchair. Dad drove the short distance to the condo slowly and with exaggerated caution while Harper slumbered peacefully next to Maggie in the back seat of the SUV.

At home, Maggie set the car seat down on the floor in the great room, unzipped the sleeping baby's snowsuit and used the remote to lower the blinds on the floor-to-ceiling windows blotting out the high-rise Chicago cityscape.

Mom beckoned her to follow into the third bedroom which she apparently had earmarked as the nursery. Amazing. Her parents had transformed the room in a few days. The walls were painted a light lavender. Maggie was drawn to the antique white crib that resembled a sleigh bed in the corner of the room. She fingered the soft lavender quilt in the crib.

"It's convertible," Mom said. "Dad put the rails in your storage unit for when she grows out of the crib."

"Wow, thanks, Mom. And you bought me a rocking chair, too!"

Maggie plopped down into the cushioned chair. "So comfortable."

She touched the purple seat cushion. "And I love the color. I love everything."

Mom beamed at her. "I kinda thought you would."

She folded her arms and gazed at the wall over the crib. "Dad did the stencil himself last night. He said if you don't like it, he can have it painted over."

Maggie burst into tears. "No…it's just perfect," she stammered.

The stencil read, *And they lived happily ever after.*

Chapter 2

December 15, Present Day

Kane Binder-Martin heard the doorbell chime but chose to ignore it. He had just moved into the sprawling beach house a week ago and had learned repeatedly how neighborly the folks were on Outer Banks. It seemed he had received welcomes from every full-time resident on the OBX sand bar the past week. Kane had enough casseroles, brownies, and cookies to feed every resident on the Banks, too.

Acting hospitable to these givers of hospitality had taken hours away from his work all week. His only reaction to the continuous doorbell ringing that morning was to refrain from playing the piano hoping the caller would believe that the house was empty and go away.

No luck. Whoever was at his door seemed determined to break the darned bell.

"All right already. I'm coming," he said to the empty room.

He shoved off the piano bench with a thrust of his legs and left the music room. Kane took the steps two at a time bounding down two flights of stairs and then jogged through the house while the doorbell chimes rang in his ears. He swung open the front door with muscle.

His cousin, Skye, stood on his porch. Her long, red hair was lit from behind by the low in the sky, morning sun casting a fiery halo around her scowling face. She balanced a cardboard box in her arms.

"It's about time, Kane. My arms are breaking," she said as she shouldered past him into the hallway.

He relieved her of the box noting its heaviness. "What's in here?"

"Enough food to feed you and your friends and lovers for days." She arched her eyebrows. "Have any of those?"

Kane huffed a laugh. "Give me a break, Skye. I've only been here six days."

Her eyes danced. "Heartthrob like you? I thought you'd have women falling all over you by now."

"Well…" he got into the game. "Women have been dropping by on a daily basis to," he made air quotes, "welcome me to the neighborhood."

"I'm sure." She looked around. "Any place where we could sit?"

"Of course. Follow me."

Kane led Skye through the yet unfurnished dining room into the rear of the house. Here he had taken great pains to equip the great room to take advantage of the reason he had built the house in that location. The entire back of the house was glass affording a glorious vista of the ever-changing sea and stretch of sand beyond his rear deck.

"Wow." Skye plopped down on the white leather sectional facing the windows. "I love this view, Kane. Amazing."

"It's inspiring. I have the same view while I work upstairs in my music room. I'm nearly done composing the score for the latest Saga movie. If the doorbell would stop ringing."

"Yeah, well, guilty." Skye propped her feet up on the slate-topped coffee table and nestled against the back cushion of the sofa. "It's lovely to take a break from chasing the triplets."

"They are the cutest kids," Kane said with a smile. "Did you get a sitter?"

"No, I dropped them at the inn with Mom. They adore their Nana, and she is so good controlling them. Makes me feel guilty for all the…challenges I gave her growing up."

"Are they always morphing into creatures and flying off like you, Bree and Summer?"

"Oh yeah. But not so much with Mom in charge. They're the worst with Gabe. He thinks it's too cool if they're pelicans or butterflies or whatever…"

"It is that. Very cool." Kane hoisted the box onto the kitchen counter, opened the flaps and unpacked the Tupperware containers and tin foil covered plates. "What do we have here?"

Skye turned her head gazing in his direction. "Anything in Tupperware goes in the fridge. Cookies, brownies, and homemade fudge are on the plates. You may or may not want to stow them in the refrigerator."

"Or the freezer." Kane opened the refrigerator door. "Want anything before I put it away?"

"No, thanks. I'm good."

Kane stashed the food in the refrigerator, skirted the counter and sat down next to Skye. He wrapped his arm around her shoulders. "So, are you hiding out here? You're welcome to relax while I work if you like."

She gazed at him her green eyes soft. "It's sweet of you to offer. And now that you live a couple blocks away from me, I may just take you up on hiding out here sometime. But today I came over with a big box of food to bribe you into coming with me to the inn to help decorate."

He nodded. "I see."

"You're nodding, yes?"

"No, I'm just nodding." Kane gave her a crooked grin.

"Come on, Kane, it will be fun."

"No, it won't," he said. "It will be a lot of work. Aunt Kay goes nuts with decorations."

"Well, that's true. But now that you live close it's so special for her to make you a part of her very favorite season. You're her favorite nephew, you know. And my favorite cousin."

Kane burst out laughing. "You are so full of it. But I could never say no to Aunt Kay." He ruffled her hair. "And you, too, favorite cousin. Count me in."

He stood up offering Skye his hand.

"Can I just keep hiding here for a little longer. It's so peaceful."

"Not a chance." He clasped her hand and tugged her upright. "The sooner we get over there, the sooner we're done."

"All right, all right." She gave him a wan smile. "I drove over here, so I didn't have to carry the box. Want a ride?"

"Nah. I'll walk the beach and meet you there."

"OK." She took a few steps away from him towards the front of the house, stopped and spun around to face him. "You're really coming, right?"

Kane chuckled. "Yes. If it'll make you feel better, you can watch me go out the back door."

"OK." She put her hands on her hips. "I'll watch."

Wagging his head, he strode to the glass doors off the great room, slid the door open, stepped out onto the deck, closed the door, and gave Skye a wave of his hand.

"See ya in a few," he mouthed.

Grinning, he turned his back on her and climbed down the stairs. He slipped off his flip flops one by one and dangled them in his hand as he set out along the sand toward the inn which was situated on prime beachfront property about six "city" blocks away from his house.

The Inn of the Three Butterflies was the stuff of legend on the Outer Banks handed down through generations of identical triplets in the Binder family dating back to the 18th century. His mother, Kamille, Aunt Karol, and Aunt Kay were identical triplets like his cousins Skye, Bree, and Summer.

A lot of unusual talents ran in his family. Aunt Kay's practical talent, along with her husband, Mike, was running the family legacy inn like a world class establishment. His mother and father along with two of his brothers ran an international branded cookie company headquartered in Chicago: Kamille's Kookies. Aunt Karol was a celebrated artist, like his cousin, Skye. Skye's identical sisters, Bree and Summer were respected in their fields, too. Bree was a pediatric psychiatrist in Chicago and Summer was a defense attorney in the New York Metropolitan area.

Kane hadn't visited OBX from Chicago as often as he'd liked growing up. But when he had spent time there, he'd always left wanting more.

His early career composing scores for feature films had taken him to California initially. A series of lucky breaks, as Kane viewed them, had brought him acclaim, awards, and the ability to name his price on projects.

Better still, he could work anywhere. He sold his California condo, bought a condo in Chicago, and found the beachfront lot on Outer Banks where his newly built dreamhouse stood.

His twin brother, Ty, lived in Kane's Chicago place since Kane wasn't willing to give it up and entirely abandon his hometown city for the beach life—maybe ever. He loved the Windy City and could afford living in the best of both worlds.

Right then, he thought he lived in the best possible world. Mid-December and the thermometer registered an exceptional seventy-five degrees. Even the coldest December day on the sand bar had Chicago's frozen tundra winters beat. He felt blessed walking barefoot on the beach with the roar of the waves and cries of the gulls—nature's music in his ears. Kane broke into a jog, exhilarated.

He arrived at the rear deck of the inn, washed sand off his feet at the spigot, slipped on his sandals and climbed the wooden steps leading to the screen porch off the rear of the main building. Kane scuffed his feet repeatedly on the rubber mat outside the patio doors before he entered the kitchen.

Inside, his ears were filled with the music of laughter and lively conversation. The place smelled a lot like his mom's bakery, redolent with buttery, cinnamon, chocolaty, mouth-watering aromas. Aunt Kay may not have owned a cookie company, but she sure knew how to bake.

Kane drifted out of the kitchen to the front parlor toward the sound of voices. Here he was met with a family tableau of three redheaded, impish, toddler girls getting into everything, their frazzled mom riding herd and his utterly serene aunt and uncle calmly hanging ornaments on a ten-foot tall, natural pine tree. The room smelled exactly like Christmas should smell—pine and cloves and cinnamon. It reminded Kane of family, togetherness, and laughter—what he encountered in his aunt's parlor.

"Kane you're here," Aunt Kay exclaimed bustling over to him to wrap him in a warm hug.

"I'm here and ready to work. Hi, Uncle Mike."

"Welcome. Feel like hanging some pine garland with me?" Mike gestured toward the lengths of garland heaped on the floor in the corner of the room.

"We have enough of the stuff to line a trail from here straight over to the Wright Memorial Bridge," Mike grumbled.

Kay fake-punched Mike's arm. "Oh you."

She turned towards Kane. "Wait until we plug in the tree, and God forbid, the lights don't work. Now that will be some championship complaining."

Uncle Mike shrugged his shoulders and hoisted up a length of garland. Kane grabbed an end and followed Mike beneath the arched entrance to the dining room where a ladder was positioned. Mike stepped to the side and Kane intuited that he was the designated ladder climber.

He had mounted the first step when a small body whizzed into the dining room beneath the garland dangling between Kane and Mike. He and Mike instinctively raised the length of pine higher as Skye ducked under the garland on a bead for the baby.

"Serenity, get back here this minute," she said with apparently no effect on her daughter.

"Catch me, Mama." The kid giggled, a contagious

sound that had Kane and Mike laughing.

"Not funny," Skye tossed over her shoulder as she and her runaway daughter disappeared into the back of the house.

Kane hooked one end of the garland in place and dismounted the ladder. Serenity's laughter intensified. Skye reappeared carrying and tickling the squirming, giggling toddler.

"If you behave, miss, your cousin will give you a candy cane," Skye promised.

"Me, too!" Scarlet shouted.

"I want one," Spring said in her soft, sweet voice.

Kane caught Skye's eye. "Is it safe for them to eat?"

"Yes," Skye said. "They're very mature candy eaters."

Kane hung the other end of the garland over the archway, climbed down the ladder, and then stepped back into the parlor. He opened a box of candy canes that were stacked on the coffee table, pulled out three and handed them out to the triplets.

Kay and Skye seated the kids in the cutest miniature bucket chairs and opened the candy wrappers.

"Suck, don't bite," Skye directed her daughters. "And don't you dare get up from your chair until I wash your sticky fingers. Got it?"

Three little heads nodded. The trio ate the candy smacking and slurping noisily. Mike tapped Kane on the shoulder. His uncle had a string of lights draped around his neck.

"Your aunt wants fairy lights on the garland. You game?"

"Sure." Kane returned to his post on the ladder and began winding the strand that Mike spooled out.

A loud buzzer sounded.

"Oops," Kay said in motion toward the foyer. "I'll go. Our guests are early."

Chapter 3

"Mommy, I can see the ocean!"

Maggie glanced at her daughter's reflection in the rearview mirror and smiled at Harper's enraptured expression. "The inn where we're staying is right on the beach. Maybe our room will have a view of the ocean."

"That would be so cool." Harper plucked the wool hat—a necessity when they had boarded the plane in Chicago—off her head, releasing jet-black curls over her shoulders. "Will we be able to see Nana and Grandpa's boat from there?"

"Oh no, sweetie. They're flying all the way across that ocean to Europe where they'll board their cruise ship."

Explaining how far away Mom and Dad were at that moment brought a stab of loneliness. Her parents had selflessly helped her the past five years since Harper was born. They babysat when Maggie had to travel for the magazine and during in-office meetings, cared for Harper during routine illnesses, sat up all night with Maggie when Harper suffered an unexplained, scary fever, and chauffeured their granddaughter back and forth to school or piano lessons, never taking time off for themselves.

They had planned to travel to dream destinations in retirement. Mom wanted to go to Spain. Italy topped Dad's wish list. But then Eileen had died, Harper was born, and they put their dreams on hold. Maggie had splurged on a Christmas present for them that year: a two-week Mediterranean cruise to Spain, France and the UK followed by a week in Venice. She would spend the holidays without her parents for the first time in her life, so Maggie had eagerly grabbed the out-out-of-town assignment at the last editorial meeting to write an article about Christmas at The Inn Of The Three Butterflies. Not that she had any competition from her colleagues to do a travel piece during the holidays.

Maggie parked the rental car in a guest spot outside the inn, opened the door and inhaled deeply the tangy ocean air. She slipped out of the seat and stretched her arms overhead working out travel kinks, and then she rounded the bumper and opened the back door for her daughter.

Harper hopped out of the car as if she were on springs. "Can I take off my coat? I'm really hot."

Her question was apparently theoretical. Harper had already stripped off her jacket and tossed it into the back seat of the car.

"We don't need our coats at all," Maggie agreed. "Let's go check in and then we can come back for the luggage."

She took Harper's hand, steered her up the wooden stairs fronting the charming Victorian building, opened the door and drew up short at the sound of a booming masculine voice.

"I'll block her from this side," he shouted.

Another man yelled, "I have her! Nope. She slipped away!"

A petite, red-haired woman stood at the front desk calmly smiling at Maggie and Harper. A barefooted, ginger-haired, toddler girl streaked into the foyer and launched herself into Maggie's arms.

"Hide Serenity," she squeaked burying her head against Maggie's neck.

Maggie's breath caught in her throat when a gorgeous, raven-haired man came roaring into the room.

"I'll find you, pipsqueak." He stopped short and stood a few feet away from Maggie, who shook her head no, hoping he intuited that the little one believed she was invisible in Maggie's arms.

"I saw a little banshee run this way. Have you seen her?" He winked and his cobalt blue eyes lit with his broad, magnetic smile.

She instantly liked the man and felt a powerful tug of attraction under his gaze. "Nope. No banshees or pipsqueaks around here."

The baby's giggles tickled Maggie's neck.

"Did you see anyone, Harper?" Maggie arched her brows at her daughter urging her to play along.

"Nuh uh." She smiled, in on the joke, and her sapphire eyes gleamed with mischief.

"Serenity, Nana is going to kill me if I don't find you before our guests come," came another bellow.

A brawny man sped into the foyer and skidded to a halt in front of Maggie. "Oops, too late."

He turned toward the woman at the desk, wearing a chagrined expression. "Sorry, Kay."

"I love you, Poppy." The little girl batted her long black lashes and beamed at him.

"Oh, you little munchkin." He held his arms out striding towards Maggie.

Serenity shifted into his embrace, and he cuddled her against his chest. "You melt my heart, little one." His gaze shifted to Maggie. "How do you do, ma'am. Sorry for the bother."

"Oh, no bother at all."

He smiled and then whisked Serenity away.

"Welcome to The Inn of the Three Butterflies. I'm Kay Layton," the lady behind the reception desk said. "My husband Mike just left with our granddaughter, Serenity, and this young man is my nephew Kane Martin."

Kane gave a half bow and grinned, his navy-blue eyes dancing. Maggie's heart skipped a beat. He was the most handsome man she had ever met. He had a rock star aura that made Maggie think she had seen him before——like in the pages of celebrity magazines.

Kay's voice interrupted her musings. "I'm hoping that the craziness of the last few minutes hasn't made you regret coming. But I understand if you turn tail and run as fast as you can."

"Please Mommy, can we stay?" Harper said.

"Of course." Maggie strode forward to the desk. "I'm Maggie Larsen and this is my daughter Harper."

Kay glanced down at paperwork on her desk. "We have a lovely oceanfront room ready for you, Ms. Larsen."

"Oh, please call me Maggie." Maggie placed her credit card on the desk. "That's wonderful. Harper and I were hoping we'd have a view of the water."

"No need for this, Maggie." Kay picked up the Visa card and handed it back to her. "We're happy to bill your magazine directly for your stay."

She peered at the computer screen. "I see here that you'll check out on January 3rd."

"Uh, no. I planned to leave the day after Christmas."

"No problem. I'll correct the reservation in our system." Kay typed a few strokes on the keyboard. "We're excited about an *In The Know* feature article. Feel free to ask any of us for whatever you need."

"Thank you, Kay." Maggie accepted the room key. "My luggage is in the car."

"I'll page Mike."

"I'll handle the luggage, Aunt Kay." Kane extended an upturned hand toward Maggie. "May I have your car keys?"

Maggie made to give him the key fob and brushed Kane's hand. Merely touching him fired a sensual surge through her that rocked her to her core. She plopped the key unceremoniously onto his palm, rapidly withdrew her hand and stuffed it into her pocket as if smothering flames.

She managed to untie her tongue and muttered, "Thanks."

Kay gave Maggie a pamphlet, *The Legend of the Inn of the Three Butterflies* and a flier listing local holiday events and happenings at the inn during the next two weeks.

"After you settle in, we can sit and talk about what you'll need from Mike and me for your article," Kay said.

"Perfect." Maggie tucked the pamphlet and flier into her tote bag and turned away from the reception desk as Kane came in with their suitcases.

"Mommy, aren't you going to ask?" Harper said.

"Sorry, sweetheart, I forgot." Maggie faced Kay. "Harper would like to continue her piano lessons while we're here. Can you refer us to a teacher who might take a temporary student?"

"Hmm. I'll have to check into that for you."

"Short of lessons, what Harper really needs is a place to practice every day. Do you have a piano here?"

"No…"

"I know a place," Kane piped up.

Kay knit her brow. "All…right. Whom should I call to set this up for my guests, Kane?"

"You're looking at him. Harper can practice in my studio."

"We don't want to impose," Maggie said.

"It's not an imposition." He squatted down to Harper's eye level. "I'd love to hear you play. Let me know when you want to practice."

"Can I come every day?" Harper proposed.

"You sure can." He stood upright. "I don't give lessons, but if you're having trouble with a particular piece, I'm confident I can help you out."

"Thank you, sir."

"Please call me Kane." He smiled. "Are you ready to see your room?"

"Are you all done with me?" Maggie asked Kay.

"Yes. Enjoy your stay."

"Thank you."

Maggie followed Kane who whispered to Harper as he rolled their suitcases past the elevator and down a hallway.

"Shouldn't we take the elevator? We're on the top floor," Maggie said.

"No, Mommy. Mister Kane is going to show us a secret way to get to our room."

The little girl looked up at him adoringly, as charmed by the man as was her mother. Maggie continued walking behind the pair inwardly grappling with her emotions. Although he was a virtual stranger, something about Kane touched Maggie's soul.

He led the way into a sunny kitchen at the rear of the inn where large windows afforded a breathtaking view of the beachfront.

"The secret elevator is over there." Kane pointed to a hall on his right.

He sidled up to the kitchen counter in front of a platter heaped with chocolate chip cookies. "But you might want to sample one of my family's well-guarded recipes before we go up to your room."

"May I, please, Mommy?"

"Sure." She selected a cookie off the platter, placed it on a napkin and handed it to Harper.

Kane gave a cookie to Maggie, and then took one for himself.

Maggie broke off a small piece and put it in her mouth. "Oh, my goodness, this is heaven." She took a big bite, closed her eyes, and enjoyed the chocolate explosion.

"Told ya," Kane said.

He gave Harper seconds and then led them down a small hallway off the kitchen, stopping in front of what looked like a closet door.

Kane stooped down and whispered audibly in Harper's ear. "You can't tell anyone about this secret elevator. Deal?"

"I promise."

He opened the door, rolled the suitcases into the rear of the small compartment, and then hoisted Harper up to a seat atop the luggage bringing an explosion of giggles from the little girl. Kane wrapped an arm around Maggie's shoulders, steered her a few steps backward into the elevator and then pulled shut the door.

Facing the door inches from her nose, tucked against Kane's side, Maggie was hyper-aware of the warmth of his body and his heady scent of musky citrus. As the elevator rose, her stomach fell, overwhelmed with his nearness.

When the car stopped, Maggie shoved open the door and rushed out. Kane lifted Harper and set her on her feet next to Maggie and then he nonchalantly rolled the suitcases past them down the carpeted hallway.

He halted at the end of the corridor and stepped aside so that Maggie could open the door. "You must really rate. My aunt usually doesn't rent out this room."

"No? Why not?" Maggie fitted the key into the lock hoping that he didn't notice the slight trembling of her hand.

"It was my cousin's room, before she got married and brought that pipsqueak you just met and her identical sisters into this world to create pandemonium."

Maggie swung open the door and was greeted with a spectacular scene beyond the wall of windows straight ahead of her. "Oh, how beautiful. Just look at that view."

She drifted inside, Harper at her heels.

"It's special." Kane placed each suitcase on luggage racks at the foot of two queen-sized beds and then took a cellphone out of the back pocket of his snug black jeans. "May I have your phone number?"

Maggie gaped at him worried that she had somehow revealed that his very presence left her weak-kneed and that she very much wanted an ongoing connection to him.

"So we can coordinate times for Harper to practice at my house," he explained.

Duh. "Yeah...sure," she stammered.

She rattled off her number. Her phone buzzed in her purse.

"That's me," Kane said. "Now you have my number, too. Just call or text me whenever you want to come over."

He headed toward the open door. "I live down the beach a short walk away. Great meeting you." Kane shut the door behind him.

****

Kane skipped using the elevator opting to barrel down the back stairs instead. He snagged another cookie passing the counter as Skye stomped into the kitchen dragging a large suitcase behind her.

"Are you going on a trip?" Kane chewed on the chocolate laden treat.

"Nope, just heading back home." She opened the refrigerator door. "It's easier to pack everything for the girls in a suitcase when I go anywhere."

Skye grabbed six sippy cups from the fridge and stuffed them in the pouch on the side of the suitcase. Kane found a plastic bag in a Lazy Susan cabinet, filled it with cookies and tucked it inside the case.

She zipped the luggage closed. He stepped in to carry the bag outside to the parking area.

"Nice ride," he joked stopping at the rear of her minivan.

"Crazy right? I never imagined I'd drive a mom car instead of my jeep."

Kane hefted the suitcase into the trunk and closed the hatch.

"Mom told me that you offered to give piano lessons to a little girl. What's up with that?"

"I didn't offer to give lessons. I said she could practice playing my piano." He leaned against the side of the van.

"Really? I'm surprised you'd let anyone into your studio, especially a kid. We were never allowed anywhere near the piano at your house growing up."

"I surprised myself when I offered. But there's something about this girl that drew me to her."

"The girl or the beautiful mother?"

"Hm. How do you know her mother is beautiful?"

"Mom filled me in. So, you think she's beautiful, huh?" Her green eyes danced.

Kane side-stepped the question. "How's Gabe doing?"

"He's great." She narrowed her eyes. "But don't think I didn't notice that you changed the subject by asking about my husband."

He persisted on the same track. "Has his mother warmed up to you yet?"

She smiled. "Surprisingly, she's done a complete turnaround since the girls were born. I even enjoy her company now. I had to deliver paintings to the gallery in Virginia last week and she offered to babysit. Do you believe it? When I got to her house, I went into the nursery and found her rocking calmly in the chair while reading to three pygmy ponies. Serenity knows how much Grammy loves her horses, so she turned herself and her sisters into little ponies."

Kane widened his eyes, amazed. "Geez. How did you handle that?"

"I didn't have to handle it at all. She finished reading the story to ponies like it was the most natural thing in the world." Skye burst out laughing. "I don't know how

Mom ever controlled me, Bree and Summer."

"Ah, but did she control you? I'll never forget the time Ty and I were camped on the beach, and you turned the three of you into pelicans. You scared the crap out of us."

"I forgot about that." She snickered. "I better go round up the little monsters so Mom and Dad can have some peace. Thanks for helping with the Christmas decorating."

"It was fun. Call if you need any help again."

Kane circled the inn out to the beach. He took his shoes off and slogged through the soft sand to the water's edge. Facing the inn, he arched his neck and gazed up at the top floor knowing somehow that Maggie watched him from her room.

Inexplicably he had felt an instant, powerful connection to Maggie and Harper. He gave a wave and then broke into a jog down the beach to his new house.

Chapter 4

"This is my daughter Skye," Kay said as a slim, striking red-haired woman ducked her head into the sitting room where Maggie, Kay and Mike had gathered for preliminary discussion of the feature article.

Maggie began to rise from her seat to greet the woman, but Skye gave her a quick wave. "Oh, don't get up. I'm just passing through. Nice to meet you. See you at dinner."

She zipped past the doorway as Maggie sat back down. "Your daughter looks so much like you."

Kay patted her auburn hair smiling demurely. "Thank you. I consider that the highest compliment."

Mike sat next to Kay on the settee facing Maggie's chair. "We have two more lovely daughters identical to Skye. And then there are Kay's identical sisters." He hung a muscled arm over Kay's shoulders.

"Don't forget the grandkids," Kay said.

"How could I? You met our darling Serenity already. She has two identical sisters. And our daughter Bree has identical triplet boys."

"Wow." Maggie juggled paperwork in her lap until she found the *Legend of The Inn of the Three Butterflies* pamphlet.

She had read the fantastical Legend after unpacking—pure woo-woo. Identical infant triplets who turned into butterflies? To escape marauding pirates, to flee a burning building and just for the fun of it through the ages? That was right up there with the mystical stories in Outer Banks Native American lore.

Maggie held up the pamphlet. "So… there's a present-day connection to these triplet baby ancestors who could turn themselves into butterflies?" She couldn't believe that those words had come out of her mouth.

Kay hooted a laugh. "Outer Banks is a magical place where fables abound. Our guests get a kick out of the tales about our inn."

Mike shot Kay a look that Maggie couldn't read. *Hmm.*

The journalist in Maggie recognized a runaround but chose not to delve deeper into the nonsense. Learning about fulfilled wishes in bottles was nonsensical enough for her. "Tell me more about the tales surrounding Christmas here."

"You read the letters?" Kay said.

"I did, thank you for providing them." Maggie patted the slim binder that Kay had left on the desk in her room containing five effusive letters about wishes floated out to sea and seemingly granted on Christmas Day. Right up there with Santa Claus. "Um…I guess I don't know what to make of them."

"Understandable," Kay said, her eyes soft.

"It strikes me as…"

"A lot of hooey?" Mike chimed in smiling affably.

"Well, yes." She handed the notebook to Kay.

"I assume you'll want to write about our guests' personal stories…what drew them here and what keeps them coming back?" Kay said.

"I…uh," Maggie stammered thrown off her game by

fables and tales. "Possibly, why?"

"Please only mention first names in your article and identify yourself clearly as a journalist for *In The Know* when you meet a guest. Also, we'd like to approve your text and any photos before publication."

"Of course. That goes without saying, Kay."

Kay rose from her seat and Mike followed suit. She gently placed a warm hand on the side of Maggie's arm. "Talk with our guests during your stay. You'll meet the author of every one of those letters during the next two weeks and you can get together with them all through the holiday here. Perhaps... Perhaps you'll simply come to know."

She handed the binder back to Maggie. "Hold on to these until you're done."

"Let's go check in on the arts and crafts project." Kay beamed at Maggie. "Your Harper was shepherding the pack of little ones making ornaments last time I checked."

Maggie wasn't surprised. Harper invariably was the teacher's helper in her class.

Mike and Kay breezed out of the room leaving Maggie undecided about which direction she'd take writing her article. She thought she had opted to do a frothy little "Christmas in..." piece. She could travel with Harper to a pretty part of the country, escape Chicago winter and ease loneliness without her parents. Her win-win-win seemed far less decisive now. Were the sweet little innkeepers perpetrating a hoax to spur business during the low season?

Maggie crossed her legs, balancing her black Moleskine notebook open on her thigh. She referenced the signatures on each of the thank you letters to make a list of interview subjects: Julie Donovan, San Diego; Carol and Bob Fiore, Knoxville; Sally and John Malloy, Pittsford; Brian O'Connell and Charles Robards, Minneapolis; Nancy and Ethan Conway, Indianapolis.

Chronologically, Julie was the first guest to claim that a Christmas wish in a bottle had come true for her—right there at the inn on Christmas day. The guests had come from diverse parts of the country and written a letter to Kay individually each year after Julie's letter.

She jotted down questions: Did Julie know them? Tell them about her claim? One wish per year? Were all these guests present "year one" when Julie's wish came true? Check guest ledgers starting back five years. Did Kay and Mike advertise nationally? If so, why hadn't she heard about this place? How did her magazine hear about the inn?

Why didn't I ask for more background at the Editorial meeting? The research team purportedly pinpointed The Inn of the Three Butterflies and its Outer Banks location because of the growing popularity of annual Christmas festivities there. Nothing was said about legends or wishes.

Maggie's enthusiasm grew at the prospect of digging in and ferreting out the truth. She scribbled a heading in her notebook: Coincidences and Magical Thinking Collide.

A pole lamp with a Tiffany shade in the corner of the room blinked on casting a kaleidoscope of pastel-colored reflections on the walls surrounding her. She heard instrumental Christmas music and the muted rumble of voices emanating from the back of the inn. Leaving her notebook and paperwork behind on her chair she strolled toward the source of the noise as the aroma of Christmas pine and roasted turkey grew stronger. In addition to infant Harper's powdery scent and the mouth-watering smell of brownies baking in the oven, the aromas of Christmas trees and Thanksgiving dinner were high on Maggie's favorites list.

Men and women wearing green, red and candy cane-colored sweaters milled around a huge dining table while holding clear mugs of eggnog and full wine glasses in hand and chatting with each other like long lost friends. Harper grinned at Maggie and then continued to help Kay clear the table filling a box with construction paper chains and star ornaments.

"Can I help with anything?" Maggie offered.

"No thanks. When you're not working for your magazine, I want you to relax and enjoy," Kay said. "Shall I introduce you around?"

"No need to bother. I'll get acquainted on my own."

"Mike has a bar set up in the kitchen. Go help yourself."

"Thanks, Kay." Maggie turned her attention to her daughter. "Want to meet everyone with me?"

Harper looked around the room. "I did, Mommy." She pointed to cluster of kids gathered on the floor beneath the Christmas tree in the great room beyond the dining room archway. "When their daddies and mommies brought them to the art class."

"Gotcha. You can go play if you like until it's time for supper."

"I have to help Miss Kay."

"We're all done here, honey. Go have fun," Kay said.

She scampered away.

Maggie spied a stack of blank name tags and a

magic marker on the buffet table. She strolled over, wrote her first name on the tag, removed the backing, and stuck it onto her sweater beneath her collar bone. In her black top and jeans, Maggie didn't look Christmassy except for the red and green border of the name tag.

She headed into the kitchen to snag a glass of wine, delighted and suddenly jittery when she spied Kane seated on a stool deep in conversation with his uncle. Maggie halted, drinking in the sight of him, her pulse accelerating. Neither of the men noticed her at first, so she could secretly ogle Kane. His jet-black hair curled around his ears and the nape of his neck. She imagined that the longish cut was a product of his being too busy to visit a barber versus a fashion statement.

He hadn't changed his clothes since that afternoon, still decked out entirely in black—jeans that fit perfectly with a tucked-in black T-shirt that emphasized the V-shape of his torso and flat abs. A white band hemmed the short sleeved-shirt snug around biceps bulges. He laughed at something Mike said, displaying a single dimple in his cheek crinkling the corners of his eyes.

Maggie didn't make a sound, but he turned his head in her direction in one swift movement as if alerted to her presence. Kane slipped off the stool and strode over to her wearing a broad smile.

On the outside, Maggie exuded practiced, calm poise. Inside he had her practically swooning.

"Hi, Maggie." Kane drew nearer.

Even the deep timbre of his voice magnetized her. "Hi, Kane." She trained her eyes on Mike.

"Mike." She nodded in greeting.

Mike waved at her.

Kane gently clasped her hand. "Come sit down.

Would you like something to drink?"

Her reaction to his touch left her needing a drink. "I would." She let him lead her over to the counter.

Maggie and Kane sat on stools facing Mike. "Do you have cabernet, Mike?"

"Indeed, I do." Mike poured the drink and handed her the full wine glass.

"Slainte." Kane clinked his half-full beer mug against Maggie's glass.

"Slainte." She took a gulp of wine relaxing a small amount in Kane's thrall.

He took a handful of peanuts from a bowl on the counter and popped a few into his mouth. "Mike tells me you live in Chicago. So do I."

"You do? Don't you live down the beach from here?"

"Yes, and yes." He chomped on the nuts drawing her gaze to his mouth.

Kane had a beautiful mouth. Full lips. Probably soft. White even teeth. The guy could be a model for her magazine—any magazine.

"I just built the beach house. I have a condo in River North fronting the Chicago River," he said.

The coincidence that they lived in the same city neighborhood stunned her. "What a small world. My condo is in River North, too."

A wide smile bloomed on those full lips. "Next time we're both in town, we have to get together."

"That would be nice."

Together. Maggie couldn't remember the last time she had thought about togetherness with a man—no less a gorgeous stranger that had her twitchy with desire. Suddenly Maggie needed air.

She stood up, wine glass in hand. Maggie didn't want to appear rude in her impulse to flee. "Would you like to sit outside for a while before dinner?"

Kane rose to his feet in answer. Mike topped off his beer and Kane plucked Maggie's glass out of her hand and carried the drinks outside. Adirondack chairs painted in bright primary colors lined the deck facing the ocean in pairs, small cocktail tables between them. Kane set down the drinks on a table and turned on the gas of a nearby warmer.

Grateful for his consideration since the evening breeze was chilly, Maggie settled in the chair feeling more grounded in his company in the dim light. "What do you do for a living?"

"I'm a composer. Movie scores."

No wonder he had a piano for Harper to use. "That's fascinating. I feel like I've seen you in the media before. But Kane Martin? I'm sorry, but I don't recognize your name."

"Professionally I'm H. Binder-Martin," he said simply.

She blinked, arching her eyebrows. *Holy cow.* "Good grief, Kane, everybody knows your work. The music from *Love Is Everything* is just beautiful. I stream that soundtrack all the time."

"Thanks," he said. "I like that score."

What an understatement from the celebrated, multi-award-winning composer who was touted as the next John Williams. "But wait. Why the initial H?"

Kane hooted a laugh. "In deference to my mom."

"I don't understand."

"No offense, but you're a journalist, Maggie. I really don't want this publicized."

"Well, now I'm really confused. But I promise I won't publicize anything about you, Kane. Have Mike and Kay told you why I'm here?"

"Uh huh. To write a feature article about Christmas at the inn."

"Exactly. I can't see why I'd publicize anything about you. So, H versus—how do you spell your name with a C or K?"

"K. My mom gave me the first name, Hurrikane when I was born. It's been a sore point for me since a kid laughed at me in pre-school."

"Oh, Kane." Maggie burst out laughing, relieved when he joined in the mirth.

"So…" He faced her, his eyes gleaming in the shadows. "If you think that's funny. My brother Ty's full first name, is Typhoon."

"Oh my gosh." Maggie doubled over exploding in laughter.

Kay poked her head out the door. "I'm so glad you two are having fun."

Maggie tried to catch her breath.

"Dinner's on the buffet table," Kay said. "Come on in whenever you're ready."

Kane offered Maggie a hand. She grabbed hold and he towed her out of the chair. Still tickled by their exchange, she grinned from ear to ear stepping into the kitchen.

"It could get ugly if you ever refer to me as Hurrikane," he whispered.

Maggie covered her mouth and snorted into her hand.

Chapter 5

Kane jolted awake, sensing that he had overslept. A pile of sheet music blocked the alarm clock's digital display on his bedside table. He swung his arm out, swept the papers onto the floor and squinted bleary-eyed at the clock.

"Oh crap." He whipped off the covers and jumped out of bed, tugging his T-shirt off over his head on the way to the bathroom.

He showered, shaved, and slipped on jeans in record-breaking time, but was still bare-chested when the doorbell rang. Putting on a yellow POLO shirt while in motion out of his room-sized closet, he hustled out of his bedroom, thundered down the stairs and jogged toward the front door, finger-combing his wet hair.

Maggie's finger was poised to press the doorbell when Kane swung open the door.

The sight of her took his breath away and revved his pulse. For a moment Kane just stared at Maggie. Her streaked-blonde hair was piled on top of her head in a messy bun and her emerald-green eyes sparkled. She and Harper wore matching green sweaters dotted with tiny, red-nosed reindeer. Maggie's shapely curves made even an ugly sweater look hot.

"Oh no. Did I have the wrong time?" She fumbled with her phone to check the text messages they had exchanged about Harper practicing on his piano.

"I'm sorry." He finally found his voice. "I overslept. No excuse but I was up most of the night working."

"We can come back another time." Maggie reached for Harper's hand and started to turn towards their car.

"No, please stay. I thought I set the alarm when I crashed, but obviously I didn't. Come in. I'll make some coffee or tea. Are you hungry? I'm sure there's something to eat in the fridge."

Maggie's smile lit her face making her appear even more beautiful. "Thank you but we already had breakfast. Your aunt puts out quite the spread. But I wouldn't turn down a cup of coffee."

"I had pancakes and waffles *and* cereal," Harper said, wide-eyed.

"I believe it, Harper. Aunt Kay is very good at overfeeding her guests." Kane stepped aside. "Come on in. First stop, the kitchen for some nectar of the gods."

He led them into his bright white kitchen. The view of the aquamarine waves pounding the shoreline through a wall of windows added the only hint of color.

"Wow." Maggie eyed the state-of-the-art appliances. "This is amazing."

"I can't take credit for the kitchen design. I gave my cousin Skye my checkbook with my permission to go crazy. From the bank statement I received I would say she did just that." He laughed. "Two rooms were off limits—my office and my studio. I worked closely with the architect on the plans, and she created exactly what I wanted."

Kane placed milk and sugar on the counter and handed Maggie an oversized mug of coffee.

"Let's get this little lady started and I can show you the rest of the house if you're interested."

"I'd love a tour," Maggie agreed.

"Oh, wow," Harper said when she reached the top floor landing. "I want a room just like this when I grow up."

Kane's music room was on the third floor of the house. All four walls were glass. The piano sat in the center of the room facing the ocean. He had designed the penthouse floor plan with his office visible through the wall to the left of the piano and a full recording studio on the other side of the glass wall opposite the office. Speakers were mounted around the room near the ceiling and sand-colored loveseats flanked the door.

He led Harper inside the music room. The glass door swished shut and sealed behind them.

"The humidity is carefully monitored and controlled in these three rooms to prevent moisture from damaging the piano and the recording equipment," he said.

Harper tiptoed over to the piano as if approaching a sleeping infant. She slid her turquoise backpack embroidered with tiny little dogs off her shoulders. Kane reached out and caught the pack on the downslide. He held it for her while she tugged on the zipper.

"Do you have a dog?" He pointed to an embroidered figure.

"Not yet. But maybe Santa will bring me one this year. I have been a very good girl all year long. A puppy is number two on my list."

"Really, what's number one?"

"I'm sorry but I can't tell you. There's a bottle in our room at the inn. And there was a note with it that explained what to do. If you write your wish on a paper and put the paper in the bottle and then throw the bottle in the ocean, your wish might come true. But you can't tell anybody your wish, or it will automatically not come true."

"All that was in the note?"

"Not the part about telling. I already know that about wishes."

"Well, I didn't. Thanks for the info."

She nodded with a serious expression on her face and then dug inside the backpack extracting a paper. He rested the pack against the bench leg on the floor as Harper set her sheet music carefully on the piano's rack. Kane leaned over Harper's shoulder for a closer look and smiled at the childish markings.

"Do you mind if I listen for a few minutes?" he said.

"I don't mind. Once I start playing, I don't notice anyone in the room. I'm working on a new piece." She took a pencil out of the side pocket of the backpack, tucked it behind her ear and sat on the piano bench.

"I'll just sit over there with your mom. If you need any help let me know."

Maggie perched on the couch. Kane stood for minute observing Harper. She closed her eyes and then her fingers flew up and down the keyboard running arpeggios in major and minor keys.

He sat down next to Maggie and their arms brushed focusing him abruptly on the mother rather than the daughter experiencing a powerful jolt of attraction.

Maggie jiggled her knee.

Kane stilled the bobbling by gently cupping her kneecap. "Don't be nervous. I won't say anything negative. I promise. She has great posture, and she's playing the chords perfectly."

"Oh, I'm not nervous."

****

Maggie wasn't anxious about Harper's performance—quite the opposite. Kane was in for a shock when she started playing in earnest. However, his hand casually resting on her knee had her nerves jangling.

Harper finished warming up and then, with her eyes still closed, started playing "Fur Elise," her favorite first-up practice song.

Kane squeezed her knee. "Is this the piece she said she was working on?"

Maggie delighted at the wonder in his voice. People usually underestimated five-year-old Harper. Not Maggie. She knew that her child was gifted since the first time her toddler fingers danced along the keys. "No. This is her warm-up piece."

His eyebrows shot up. "Warm up? Do you have any idea just how hard "Fur Elise" is to play correctly? And she's playing correctly."

Maggie laid her hand over his. "You, Mr. Martin, are in for a treat."

****

Harper shuffled her sheet music and then launched into playing a different piece. Kane couldn't sit still. He stood up and stepped behind Harper focusing on the little dots on the sheet of paper on the rack: a child's handwriting with no significance that jumped out at him. The song she played was lively yet haunting. He had never heard the melody before.

Kane turned around, walked over toward Maggie, and stood in front of her. "Do you know the name of the song she's playing?"

"I don't think she's given it a name yet. She likes to finish a piece before she thinks of a name, and then moves on to the next composition."

"What?" He raised his voice, dumbstruck. "Are you telling me that she composed this music?"

Harper stopped playing and swiveled on the bench gaping at him. "Did I do something wrong?"

"Oh, no. Not at all." He smiled at the pretty little girl. "I'd say you're doing everything right. I'm sorry I interrupted."

"That's OK. I keep getting this far, and I'm not sure where to go next."

"It happens to me, too." He sat down on the bench next to her. "Tell me about this piece."

"Well… I started it when Mommy said we were going to the ocean. I was happy but then I was sad because we wouldn't be with Nana and Grandpa for Christmas. So, it started happy but then got sad."

"You're thinking that you don't know how this trip is going to end. Right?"

"Yes. That's it."

"As one composer to another, if it were me, I would finish the way I hoped the trip would end. In your case, with Santa bringing a puppy and your wish coming true."

He winked at her and peered at the sheet music. With the echo of what she had played in his mind, suddenly the dot system she used made sense to him. "Maybe something like this…"

****

Maggie fixated on his long fingers moving rapidly along the keyboard. The room swelled with gorgeous music, a variation of Harper's song.

"Now that is how I might end the piece." He elegantly raised his fingers off the keys and placed them in his lap.

"Oh, I love that!" Harper immediately replayed the song exactly as had Kane but added her own flourish at the end. A sweet smile bloomed on her face as she hugged him. "Thank you, that's what I will do."

Maggie was impressed by Harper's open display of affection for him. Harper withdrew at times and typically had to know someone very well before she doled out hugs. But what impressed her more was the joyful expression on Kane's face as he hugged her daughter back. Could he possibly behave any better? She hardly knew the man and she was already half in love with him.

He slid off the bench and ambled towards Maggie holding out his hand. "Do you want that tour now?"

She accepted the handhold and rose from her seat. "Shouldn't we wait until Harper is finished practicing? She usually plays a couple hours a day. I should stay and supervise her using your piano."

"Not necessary on my part. Let's ask her."

Harper had resumed playing. From experience, Maggie knew she had shut them and everything else but the music out.

"Harper?" Kane said.

No answer.

He curved his index finger and thumb into a mouth harmonica and blew a whistle riveting Maggie's attention on his full lips.

Harper opened her eyes and turned her head towards him, questions in her eyes.

"Can I give your mom a tour of the house while you play?"

She gave him a head nod and then scribbled something on her sheet of music.

"There are speakers on the walls. We'll hear you

playing throughout the house. We'll also hear you if you call us."

"OK," she mumbled without taking her eyes off the paper.

Kane still clasped Maggie's hand. He led the way out of the studio.

"You have an amazing daughter. Is your husband musical?"

"I'm not married." She followed him into his office.

The loaded bookcases along the back wall captured her attention—more for the gleaming awards that served as bookends than his literature collection.

"Does Harper's dad support her music?" he said.

"Harper's dad is not in her life. Wow," she said. "I have never seen a Tony or an Oscar in person. These are amazing. All you need is an Emmy and a Grammy, and you'll be an EGOT."

"I have a couple of Grammys. They're around here somewhere. But I'll tell you what's amazing. Your daughter is amazing."

Maggie picked up on his change of subject. He obviously didn't like to talk about himself.

"When did you notice Harper had such huge talent?"

"To be honest I never thought much about it. She taught herself to read at three and the next thing I knew she was playing the songs she heard on *Sesame Street* on the piano by ear. No one in my friend group had children, so to me this was all normal. When she started Pre-K, I realized that she was different."

"Funny. If you asked my mom, she would probably say the exact same thing about me. I started playing by ear as a toddler, too."

He led her downstairs to the second floor. Kane

stood in front of her, so close that she could smell his citrusy cologne. Maggie's heart thudded in her chest and her surroundings blurred as he cupped her face in his warm hands.

"I have wanted to kiss you since the first time I saw you at the inn, but I didn't know until today that you're single. May I kiss you?"

"I would like that very much," she whispered, barely able to form words.

His eyes shimmered and his lips touched hers gently. Maggie melted into the kiss as he took her into his arms.

"Mom! I have to go to the bathroom." Harper's voice blared through a nearby speaker.

Maggie's eyes flew open. She pulled away from Kane. He burst out laughing.

"I'm sorry." Maggie's face flushed as they climbed the stairs.

"Nothing to be sorry about, but I definitely want a raincheck."

Chapter 6

She turned her head for just an instant to check on Harper playing in the sand at the water's edge. The wave crashed over Maggie's head and tossed her into a cyclone of disorienting turbulence. To make matters worse she had opened her mouth to shout out a greeting to her daughter when the ocean upended her. Gagging, she tried to remain calm while she somersaulted, scraped along the sandy bottom, and then was hurled presumably away from the shore. Her inner compass wasn't functioning, and her lungs burned lacking oxygen. *If I could just gain my footing.*

****

Maggie opened her eyes, the frothy water a stinging abstract of bubbles and swirls in her field of vision, which did nothing to point her in the right direction. A vice-like grip around her midriff hoisted her upward. She surfaced dangling within that grip spitting out briny water and then sucking in a lungful of air.

"I've got you," came the bass voice of her rescuer.

Kane, bless him, lifted her, cradled her in his arms and sloshed through the seemingly calm, rolling swells onto the beach where Harper, Skye and her gaggle of toddlers lined up staring at her.

Maggie rested her head against Kane's chest, shaken and grateful that he had somehow magically known that she was in trouble. "How?"

"Shh," he soothed. "Let's get you comfortable on your beach blanket."

He gently set her down and then hunched over her, his large body eclipsing the bright sun, a penumbra shadowing his face. "Has your breathing regulated?"

She blinked and nodded, yes. "I'm all right."

Maggie twisted around and opened the cooler on the sand at the edge of the blanket. She dug inside, plunged her hand into ice cubes, grabbed a sweating bottle of water, and glugged half a bottle to get rid of the fishy, salty residue in her mouth.

Wiping her lips with the back of her hand, she sighed. "Better." She gazed deeply into Kane's eyes, the color of the ocean she had just narrowly escaped. "Thank you so much for saving me. I didn't have much breath left. Where did that wave come from? The water was so calm when I waded in. You'd think I'd follow my own advice to Harper."

"Never turn your back on the ocean," Harper piped up. "I was so scared, Mommy. I saw you go under but then the most wonderful thing—"

"Hey, Harper!" Skye interjected. "Want to help the girls fill buckets so we can build an awesome sandcastle?"

"Um…sure. Can I tell Mommy about the giant pelican first?"

Kane turned his head toward his cousin. Skye met his eyes and a message, or a warning flashed between them that Maggie couldn't decipher.

Skye circled her arm around Harper's shoulder. "Let's let your mommy rest a bit," she said. "I want to build an epic castle."

"Cool." Harper scurried away with Skye as Kane sat

down next to Maggie.

He rested his elbows on bent knees and hung his head pulling Maggie's focus to the taut muscles in his calves and thighs covered with sable hair and the sopping wet swim trunks and short-sleeve T-shirt molded to the ridges and chiseled planes of his body. A thrill of sheer lust swept through her that had her marveling at the fate that had brought her there. She had no idea when she had decided to flee holiday loneliness in Chicago that she would wind up a gorgeous, talented man's damsel in distress.

Kane tilted his head toward her, his navy-blue eyes dancing. "I guess you're not in the mood for a swim."

Maggie threw back her head laughing, and he joined in. She caught her breath. "I'd love to stroll the beach, though. Feel like shelling on this famous shell beach your aunt touted at breakfast this morning?"

"Sure." He shrugged off his shirt and plopped the sopping cloth on the blanket. Flexing his legs, he stood upright in one fluid movement and extended a handhold to Maggie.

His large hand encompassed hers and he towed her to her feet with muscular ease. "Hey Harper," he hollered.

Harper knelt in the sand wielding a toy shovel amid the chaos of erecting a sandcastle with three toddlers. She raised her head. "Yeah?"

"Want to go shelling with me and Mom?"

"No, thanks. Can I stay here with Miss Skye and the girls?"

"Yes. Just mind what Miss Skye says," Maggie said.
"Uh huh."

Maggie looped a large net bag over her arm. "I'm on

a quest for a Scotch bonnet."

"Pretty rare but not impossible. Let's hunt."

She entwined her fingers in his and strolled the beach feeling exhilarated and lucky that Kane had somehow been there exactly when she had needed him.

****

Kane had reached the crest of the sand dune revealing the panorama of Shell Beach when a rogue wave knocked Maggie off her feet. He had whipped his head toward Skye navigating the soft sand next to him, her babies in tow holding her hands. "Skye, help. I'll never reach her in time."

Skye had simply nodded, dropped the girls' hands, and clutched his. She had beseeched the Sacred Source in binding the spell. Kane had experienced the full body jolt of metamorphosis raising his arms, transformed into a wide wingspan. The huge black pelican had soared over Harper's head and had dived straight into the height of a cresting wave.

He hadn't tapped into Skye's Sacred Source-given power since he was a tween, but he had never forgotten her most critical tutorial: how to employ his family's unique abilities and unbind one of her spells. His body had shuddered, and his blood had thundered in his veins as bird had become man once again.

Luck had it that the undulating water had rushed Maggie practically into his arms. He had grabbed hold of her by the waist, anchored his feet firmly in the ocean's sandy bottom and stood up yanking Maggie above the surface. When she had sputtered and sucked in air, he had expelled a huge breath of relief.

His nerves still jangled on the adrenaline high as he strolled the beach next to her. She stooped occasionally to scoop up a shell here and there, inspecting, rejecting, and stowing favorites in her bag.

"I'll carry your bag," he volunteered.

"Thanks." She handed it over, a sweet smile blooming on her lips. Even with her wet, blonde hair slicked back off her face devoid of makeup she looked beautiful. Her demure forest green, one-piece bathing suit molded to her perfect body and brought out the emerald color of her eyes.

Kane gazed at the sand as he ambled helping her search for shells. "Straight ahead. There's a whelk in that backwash."

She dropped his hand and raced into the shallow water where the ebbing wave sucked at the glistening shell. Scooping up her prize as the receding water buried her toes in the wet sand, she raised it overhead exultantly beaming him a wide smile.

"It's perfect," she said.

He held the bag open for her. She skipped over to him, clunked the shell into the bag and then fell into pace with Kane strolling along the beach, heads bent to the random luck task of finding perfect seashells. He hoped he would find her an elusive Scotch bonnet so he might earn another joyous Maggie smile. Kane shuddered to think of how close he had come to losing her. If Skye hadn't come with him to the beach, could he have reached Maggie quickly enough?

He marveled at how special to him Maggie had instantly become. The too brief kiss she had granted him at his house had tantalized him. Kane wanted more. Much more.

"Do you get to come shelling here a lot?" she said. "I saw that huge jar of seashells in your powder room."

"Not really. Skye and her sisters, Bree, and Summer filled that jar. I'm usually holed up in my studio all day. Except for sunrise walks on the beach."

"I love sunrise walks—especially near the ocean. You're so lucky."

"I'd be luckier if you came with me. Would you like to?"

"Oh yes."

"It's a date."

There was that joyous Maggie smile. He set the bag down on the sand and drew her into his arms. Kissing her there with a soft breeze caressing his back and shoulders and her body pliant in his embrace felt right—destined, perfect.

"Um…" She looked up at him, a dazed expression on her lovely face. "What was that for?"

Kane grinned at her. "Pretty woman, pretty day. I'm feeling lucky that she gave me a kiss."

"I'm pretty sure you took that kiss."

"Oh yeah? Seems like you gave it back."

She chuckled. "It was a pretty good kiss."

The clamor of children's voices sounded. Two kids crossed their path on a bead for the ocean.

Kane clasped Maggie's hand and reversed direction. "To be continued."

"Yes," she said.

"Tell me more about you, Maggie. I know you're a journalist, of course. Do you like the work?"

"I love what I do," she said. "I've always loved to write. It's such a blessing for me to earn a living from my passion and have the flexibility to be with Harper."

"I get that," he said. "She's an amazing kid."

"She is my heart. And she hero worships you

already, Kane. Thank you so much for opening your studio to her."

"My pleasure. Really. She impressed the hell out of me."

"Thanks. I'm real proud of her."

"As you should be." He gazed out at the ocean.

The sun sparked diamond glints on the aqua, glassy surface of the water and a scrim of pelicans glided above the swells. A pair of gray-black dorsal fins rolled atop a cresting wave and then the dolphin pair came more fully into view surfing not more than ten feet offshore.

He pointed at the spectacle. "There, Maggie. You see the dolphins?"

She trained her eyes along the length of his arm. "Oh wow! Darn, I forgot my phone to take a photo. I wish Harper were here to see this."

Knowing Skye's "talents" communing with sea creatures, he felt sure Harper would experience some magical connections while in his cousin's company. "How long is your stay here?"

Her eyes met his. "Until the twenty-sixth. But my article is due to my editor on Christmas Eve. She wants to run it in the special Christmas edition of *In The Know*. My parents are on a cruise during the holidays so there's not much waiting for Harper and me at home."

"Your ex doesn't want to spend any holiday time with his daughter?"

She dropped her eyes. "I've never married, so nope, no ex to share Harper with."

When she met his gaze, a fleeting shadow seemed to shimmer in her green eyes. "Someday I'll tell you the story."

Instinctively he clasped both her hands. "Is it sad,

Maggie?"

She remained quiet.

"I don't mean to pry…"

"It's OK." She tugged him gently into resuming their walk. "It's… well, it's better left to another time. How about you, Kane? Were you ever married?"

"No, ma'am."

"Commitment-phobic, are you?" she teased.

He smiled. "Not at all. Just no relationships that have led in that direction." *Until I met you.*

"I can't resist asking. If the right woman came along, would you settle down?"

"Sure."

"What about kids? Do you want a family?"

"I love kids. I want to steal Serenity, Scarlet, and Spring right out from under Skye's nose."

Maggie burst out laughing. "Wow, you do love kids."

"So back to you," he said. "You're writing about Christmas at the Inn of the Three Butterflies?"

"Yes. Now, possibly focusing on the legend about wishes in a bottle."

"Hmm." Kane had a brainstorm. "Considering yours and your daughter's creative talents, do you think you two might collaborate with me?"

Maggie halted in her tracks and gazed at him wide-eyed. "What do you mean?"

"I think you've probably picked up on the fact that my cousin, Skye, is a force to be reckoned with."

She knit her brow. "Uh huh."

"Well, Skye has strong-armed me into the role of the musical director for the village Christmas concert this year. I'm working on an original holiday melody—

tentatively entitled Magic Christmas Bells. I'd like to orchestrate the song for a piano duet with Harper."

"Wow! She's going to flip. Of course, I approve. Let's hurry back to tell her." She set in motion, but Kane gently tugged her hand to bring her to a stop.

Maggie faced him wearing a quizzical expression.

"I'm no lyricist. Would you consider putting words to my music? In addition to conducting the municipal orchestra, Skye has me working with the children and adult choruses." He wagged his head wondering how Skye had managed to sweet-talk him into the responsibility in the first place.

"Wow again, Kane. I'm flattered. But I've never written song lyrics before. I'm not sure I'd be any good at it."

"No pressure." He resumed strolling the beach. "But I think it would be pretty special if you agreed." He huffed a laugh. "Not to mention that I might actually enjoy the whole thing if you and Harper were involved."

"I agree, it would be beyond special. I promise I'll give my part some thought. Let's go tell Harper. She'll be so excited."

Chapter 7

"I'm sorry, Harper. I know you were looking forward to watching the parade of boats with Skye and the little ones, but Kane texted that he had a surprise for us. He's been so generous letting you practice on his piano that I just couldn't say no."

Maggie secretly thrilled at Kane's invitation whatever he had in mind. Spending time with him had made her stay on Outer Banks delightful.

"I really wanted to see the boats, but I do love surprises." Harper's grin warmed Maggie's heart. *She's such a good girl.*

She checked the weather app on her phone. The temperature had dipped twenty degrees lower from the balmy mid-seventies earlier in the day. "Kane said to dress warm. Let's bring coats, hats, and scarfs."

Their jackets and gloves fitted into her over-sized backpack after she rolled and wedged them inside. Maggie held up two pairs of matching scarves: one dotted with green Christmas trees and the other with gnomes sporting Santa hats. "Which ones?"

"The gnomes. It's my favorite."

She handed Harper the scarf of choice, wrapped hers around her neck and stowed the other two in the closet.

A text signal sounded as Maggie tugged the backpack's zipper closed. "It's from Kane," she said. "We better go. He's running late and wants us to meet him at his house."

Maggie chuckled reading the last couple lines of his text.

—The alarm is set. Just type in 1234 to turn it off. I know, I know, but I haven't had time to change it and be honest, a burglar wouldn't think someone could be stupid enough to use that code. See you soon. Can't wait.—

It was a quick drive over to his home. Just inside the door, Maggie keyed in the supplied code on the wall panel and the alarm's beeps subsided.

Strains of music emanated from speakers on the first floor. Maggie stood there enjoying listening to him play the piano. A soprano voice began singing with his accompaniment.

The music cut off abruptly and Kane's voice boomed, "Let's try it again from the chorus."

"You got it, honey," a husky female voice answered.

"Mom," Harper whispered, "doesn't that sound like Carly Thomas?"

"It does. I wonder..."

He played a few bars on the piano and then a guitar accompanied him. Her soprano and a harmonizing baritone sang lyrics about first kiss, first love, first touch, first... There was a break in the music. The woman sighed and then came the strains of a solo guitar.

A few beats of silence were broken when Kane said, "That's it. That was perfect, Carly."

Harper tugged at Maggie's sleeve. "I told you, Mom. That *is* Carly Thomas, I just know it!"

"You are perfect, love," Carly said. "I refuse to record this song for the movie unless you duet with me."

Kane's hearty laugh echoed in the house. "I write

the songs; I don't sing them."

"Ah, but you'll make an exception for me, won't you honey? I can be very persuasive."

"I'll think about it, but right now I'll end our zoom session. A very special lady is waiting for me."

"Should I be jealous?"

"Would a five-year-old girl make you jealous?"

"No, I don't think so."

"How about her beautiful mother?"

"Well, that might. Who is this beautiful lady?"

"Merry Christmas, Carly. I have to go."

Footsteps thundered from above and then he appeared bounding down the stairs and beaming at Maggie.

Elation surged through her at the sight of his handsome face and his description of her as beautiful. He certainly made her feel beautiful.

"I'm sorry you had to drive over here. I intended to pick you up. But my session ran long. Thanks for being flexible," he said.

"Was that Carly Thomas singing?" Harper said, a wonderstruck expression on her face.

"Yes, it was. Do you like her music?"

"I love her music. Mommy said when her tour comes to Chicago, we'll go."

"I said I would try," Maggie corrected. "I've tried and failed before to get tickets to her concerts."

"I'm pretty sure I can help there." Kane winked at Harper. "I know her."

"That would be so cool. If you sing your song with her like she asked, she'll probably give you tickets," Harper said.

Maggie and Harper fell into step beside Kane

leaving the house.

"I didn't know you sang," she said pausing at the side of his SUV.

"I don't generally." Kane opened the passenger and rear doors for them. "But the song's a duet and I jumped in for the run through."

Maggie helped Harper with her seatbelt and then slipped into the front seat.

"You should sing that song with Carly for her movie. You sounded so good, and I really want tickets," Harper chattered.

Kane hooted a laugh. "Enough about my mediocre voice. It's time for your surprise."

He drove over a bridge and pointed to the boats lined up at the dock in Pirates Cove. The sun dipped below the horizon trailing bands of magenta and fiery orange. Almost in unison strings of lights adorning the boats switched on—multicolored starbursts amid the gathering darkness.

"Oh wow!" Harper said. "Are these the boats for the parade?"

"Exactly." He pulled into one of the last parking spaces and opened the doors for Harper and Maggie. "We've been invited to ride in the parade. Come on."

"Oh, wow," Harper crowed.

Kane stepped between them, clasped Harper's and Maggie's hands and walked briskly along the pier. He pointed to a sleek, sport fishing boat encrusted with Christmas lights fore and aft. "That's our ride. It belongs to my friend, Harley."

"Did I hear my name?" A burly man wearing a Santa hat, a bit small for his large head, yelled down from the boat's upper mezzanine."

"You sure did, Harley. Permission to come aboard?" Kane said.

"Permission granted."

Harley climbed down the ladder. Kane helped Maggie and Harper board the boat, made the introductions and Harley shook everyone's hands.

"I've known Kane and his family since he was your age, Harper. My two boys couldn't wait until they came from Chicago for the summer. Your new house is beautiful, Kane. I drove by it last week on my way to the inn. How does it feel to be back?"

"It feels right. I missed the sandbar. I'll still have to travel occasionally. And I hope to spend more time in Chicago in the future, too." He shot a glance at Maggie, thrilling her.

"But the Outer Banks feels like home now," Kane said.

"It's good to have you back." Harley clapped his giant mitts together. "Would you like some hot chocolate?"

"Sure," Harper sang out.

Maggie frowned at her daughter.

"I mean, yes, please," she corrected under her mother's penetrating gaze.

That's better.

Harley clasped Harper's hand and led her to the stern. Maggie and Kane trailed behind him.

"Help yourself," he said gesturing toward a table covered with a red plastic cloth set with a platter of cookies, cheese, crackers, and a large silver urn.

Harper grabbed a frosted Christmas cookie and bit off a chunk. Maggie poured a mug of hot chocolate and handed it to her little girl.

"There's some wine in the galley if you'd like a glass or two," Harley offered.

Boat horns filled the night apparently triggering the lead boat to blare Christmas music.

"That's my cue to get to the bridge. Make yourselves comfortable."

"Do you need any help, Harley?" Kane said.

"Thanks, but I have my crew on board. Just relax and enjoy the ride."

"Would you like a glass of wine?" Kane said.

"I'd love one," Maggie said.

"Be right back." He descended the ladder to the galley.

Maggie filled a plate with cookies, cheese cubes and crackers and carried it to a table in front of a small couch.

Kane returned with two full glasses of wine and joined Harper and Maggie on the couch. The boat glided away from the dock. Harper bounced in her seat with excitement as the parade headed out into the sound.

The lighted decorations on decks and balconies and in windows of houses and condo buildings cast rainbow reflections on the water. People waved as they sailed past. Harper ran to the rail and waved back.

"Look, Mommy!" Harper pointed to a group of people under strings of red and green lights. "It's Skye and the girls!"

Maggie and Kane joined Harper at the railing. Kane put two fingers in his mouth and whistled. The triplets caught sight of them and started yelling and waving. Kay and Mike had set up a picnic for the guests. Harper beamed as they all waved and shouted hello to her.

After they passed the group, Maggie and Kane sat back down.

Harper spun around on a beeline for Kane. She threw her arms around his neck. "This was the best surprise ever," she said her eyes gleaming. "Thank you so much. This is going to be the best Christmas ever."

Kane pulled Harper in for a hug smiling at Maggie over the crown of Harper's head. Maggie's breath caught in her throat watching him connect with her daughter. She had powerful, unprecedented feelings for him that she could only define as love. She had never fallen in love before with anyone. How could she fall in love this quickly with a virtual stranger?

"Hey Harper!" Harley boomed. He clambered down the ladder panting. "We're about to pass the judges' table on the boardwalk in Duck. I need everyone cheering and festive."

He fiddled with a necklace of Christmas ornament bulbs switching on the lights and held it out to Harper. "Would you wear this and come up to the bridge with me? I really want to win this year."

"May I go with Mr. Harley, Mom?"

"You certainly may. We want to hear you cheering. We'll cheer, too."

Harley clasped Harper's hand leading her to the ladder while belting out "We Wish You a Merry Christmas" at the top of his lungs. Harper giggled and then sang loudly with him as she climbed up to the mezzanine.

Maggie gazed at Kane. "Best Christmas ever. Uh oh," she groaned. "That's a high bar. I might have to rethink the books and the LEGO set I have packed as Christmas gifts for her."

Kane laughed and put his arm around Maggie's shoulder. A cool breeze blew off the sound and Maggie snuggled within his warm embrace.

"Do you remember your best Christmas ever?" he said brushing a kiss on her crown.

"My first Christmas with Harper was magical. My best Christmas as a kid is a close second. My sister Eileen and I woke up before our mom and dad on Christmas morning. We tiptoed downstairs and searched among the presents for what we both wanted most from Santa, disappointed that he had let us down. But...when we went back to our room, the cutest puppy with a red and green bow around his neck sat on our bed wagging his tail. We squealed with joy. My dad ran into our room rubbing his eyes as if we had awakened him and asked us what was going on."

Maggie smiled. "My dad is such a good man. We named the puppy Karlie, and he was our best friend for fifteen years. There are times I still miss him. What about you? Do you remember your best Christmas ever?"

"Our stories are very similar. My best Christmases were always spent at the inn. One year our flight from O'Hare was delayed because of a snowstorm. It was a real nightmare for my parents. Predictably my brothers and I were fighting, and my sister was acting the spoiled princess. Dad threatened to call a cab, take us home and cancel Christmas when the snow stopped suddenly, and the sun came out. Everyone on our plane said it was a Christmas miracle."

"Did you think it was a miracle?"

"Well...I wouldn't rule anything out. So, we get to the inn and as always Aunt Kay and Uncle Mike make it magical for everyone. My aunt Karol was there that year, too. She always gave the best gifts. My brothers got sneakers that they had yearned for, and my sister received a doll that was number one on every little girl's wish list and was impossible for parents everywhere to find. When I opened my gift, I was crushed but tried not to show it. What was a kid supposed to do with gift cards for fast food and gasoline? I thanked her anyway—my mother would have killed me if I forgot my manners.

"After all the gifts were opened, we sat around the table and ate dessert. Aunt Karol sat next to me and asked what I thought of my gift. I love my aunt Karol. She's my godmother, and I've always been her favorite. But I couldn't lie just to be polite. I told her I didn't understand her gift. And then she told me I hadn't opened her other box. I didn't know there were two boxes. I followed her into the kitchen and sitting in an open box was the cutest Boston terrier puppy. Aunt Karol then explained that just the two of us were going to drive home to Chicago with Abigail, the puppy. The gift cards were for us to eat and fuel the car on our trip. I don't know what the best part of the gift was, a new puppy or spending time with Aunt Karol on that drive."

"I bet someday when Harper is asked about her favorite Christmas, she'll mention this boat ride. Thank you for doing this for her," Maggie said.

"You're welcome. But I had an ulterior motive." He cupped her face with his hands and gazed into her eyes. And then he dipped his head and kissed her.

When their lips met Maggie was lost in the heady connection. He deepened the kiss, and she responded equally leaving her breathless when he gently withdrew.

"Best Christmas ever," he said.

"Mm…for me, too."

"Am I going to have to buy Harper a puppy for her to agree with her mother?"

Maggie burst out laughing. "Probably."

Chapter 8

"Take it again from the coda," Kane directed Harper.

The kid dove right in playing the intricate piece. Harper impressed him, hell she staggered him, with her nuance in interpreting his music. Her sight-reading skills were off the chart. He had a metronome at the ready, but she hadn't needed to use it. She had sailed through playing the melody, which neither she nor anyone but him had ever heard before, as if it were as familiar as "Jingle Bells."

Kane's keyboard compositions were typically melody lines preceding orchestration for his signature soaring scores. When he played nascent compositions on his piano, he heard in his head the future strains of violins, cellos, flutes, horns, and percussion that would set his melodies to flight. Sometimes he'd write a song specific to a musician and vocalist, like Carly Thomas. He'd tailor the music to the singer's range and instruments played—in her case three octaves and guitar. Carly had written the lyrics to the love song that would be recorded as a duet.

Maybe that had inspired Kane to think duet when he had composed the piece that Harper was playing solo at that moment. He sat at the gleaming additional grand piano facing her that he had installed in his music room with the new composition in mind. Kane itched to get into the duel with Harper now that she had proven that she might master her part.

She dropped her hands into her lap and sighed. "That is so pretty. Almost like church or the angels or something."

Kane smiled. "I'm glad you like it. You played it very well. It's called "Magic Christmas Bells.""

Harper nodded. "Yep. Just what it sounds like. Magic bells. Can I play it again, or should I do my exercises and the Chopin I've been working on?"

"I hope your mom won't be mad if I interfere with your usual practice session, but how about we focus on this song today? We don't have much time before the concert."

"Sure." She positioned her hands over the keys. "From the beginning?"

"Hold up a sec." He rose from the bench and replaced her sheet music with pages that he had annotated for the duel.

She squinted at the first page and pointed to a notation. "What does this mean?"

"When you get to that mark, pause for two bars. I'll come in then."

"You mean we'll play together? Oh boy."

"Yes. But it's almost like we'll play music tag with each other. It's called dueling. A little like a piano duet. Used to be a competition between pianists to outplay each other."

"Wow. I could never play better than you."

Kane huffed a laugh. "Don't be so sure. Would you like to play together?"

She nodded eagerly making her long, black ponytail wag. "Oh yes."

Her blue eyes danced, and her pretty face lit with a sweet smile.

"Great. Watch my hand before beginning." He raised his right hand and made shapes in the air as if conducting the orchestra establishing the beat and cadence. "Begin," he said.

Characteristically, Harper dove right into the music. She made a couple of flubs here and there, but when corrected she always retained his instructions. Dueling with her, his respect for her talent magnified. She neither complained nor apologized for her mistakes. Instead, she persisted in executing on a par with him. The little girl was determined to meet the challenge.

His instincts about her were spot on. She was more than a natural born musician; she was also a natural born performer. Hopefully, she would be as comfortable on stage as she was in his private music room. Kane's plan to spotlight her in the town's Christmas Eve concert appealed to him more and more.

His instrumentation had her playing the last note, but she kept going an additional bar in C8: a rapid, muted tinkling of the highest notes like an echo of sleigh bells in the far distance.

"What was that?" He gazed into her wide sapphire eyes rimmed with lush, long eyelashes.

She shrugged. "I don't know. I thought maybe it needed that."

"Wow. I think you're right." Kane was blown away.

He made a quick notation of the final bar on his sheet music and then met her eyes again. A chill ran through him at the powerful tug of connection between them as if their kindred spirits bonded them. Strange. Because he felt a similar magnetic connection to Maggie as if they were meant to be bound together.

This little girl had so much in common with five-year-old Kane right down to her ability to compose music as well as play the piano—echoes of his reputation as a child prodigy. He loved kids in general, but she already occupied a special place in his heart.

Maggie…Kane sensed that she might come to own his heart entirely. Maybe she did already.

"Can we play it one more—"

The loud doorbell chime interrupted Harper.

Kane grinned at her. "Next time. Let's not keep Mom waiting."

Harper popped up off the bench and he rose to meet her at the music room door. He opened the door for her and then stepped outside into the hall. Kane pushed the intercom button on the wall and spoke into the microphone. "Door's open, Maggie. We'll be right down."

"Beat ya," he dared Harper in motion toward the stairs.

She zipped past him giggling.

"Hold on to the banister," he said fearing his proposed race down two flights of stairs might display poor guardianship to the doting mother waiting down in his foyer.

Sure-footed and obediently holding on to the railing as directed, Harper zoomed down the stairs ahead of him pulling up in front of her mother a good deal less out of breath than Kane.

"Whoa." Maggie wobbled slightly as Harper threw her arms around her waist and hugged.

Harper looked up at Maggie. "I had the best time. Kane wrote a magic Christmas bells song, and he taught me to duet. I mean duel. And I thought up a finish, and Kane liked it, and then he wrote it down, and it's really pretty, and can we play it for Mom, Kane?"

Maggie arched her eyebrows. "Sweetie, take a breath. What's all this, Kane?"

"Well," he said. "That more or less summarizes Harper's practice session today. We're working on the song for the concert."

"Ah, right. "Christmas Bells.""

""Magic Christmas Bells,"" Harper corrected.

"Got it." Maggie knit her brow. "I'm sorry, Kane. I haven't given a thought to writing the lyrics for you."

"No problem. Let us know if you think you might want to give it a try and we'll play for you."

"That would be great. Maybe tomorrow…" she bit her lip. "I'm sorry but I think I'm booked tomorrow morning with interviews. The next day?"

"Don't worry about it. I'm happy with the piece as an instrumental for the concert. The choirs can sing traditional carols."

"If you're sure…"

"I am. Can you stay for a while? I'm ready for a break. Would you like a cup of coffee or a soft drink?"

"Can I have a pop, please?" Harper said.

Maggie ruffled Harper's hair. "Yes. That's if Mister Kane has pop."

"I do."

Harper made a beeline for the kitchen. Kane and Maggie followed her.

He opened the refrigerator, supplied Harper with a can of her favorite soda which he had stocked purposely, and took a glass out of a cabinet for her while Maggie poured two mugs of coffee.

"Let's go sit on the deck," he proposed.

Outside, Harper deposited her drink on the table, slipped out of her sandals and left the deck to play in the sand. Maggie took a seat across from him and daintily sipped coffee eyeing him over the rim of her mug.

"Harper is the bright spot in this whole concert thing. Why I give in to Skye's nagging is a mystery," he complained. "She says that the annual event needs elevation, and according to her only I can do that." He rolled his eyes.

Maggie's jade eyes shone. "She's pretty convincing, huh?"

He snorted. "Like a sledgehammer. Anyway, I'm officially directing the kids' choir, the adult choir—who incidentally don't sound half as good as the kids—and the municipal orchestra for a sing along. Skye also wants me to perform. Since you've given permission, I'll only perform with Harper. I plan to spotlight her."

"She'll be honored. I can't wait to go to this concert."

He chuckled. "I'm pretty sure your daughter will carry the evening."

Maggie twisted her lips. "Oh, Kane. I don't know. Isn't that too much pressure for a five-year-old?"

"Frankly, I don't think she'd feel any pressure at all. She is poised way beyond her years at the keyboard."

She set down her mug, a pensive expression on her face. "Well. She has played in a recital, and she wasn't nervous at all."

"I think she'll amaze you. She certainly has amazed me. I promise I'll work closely with her to make sure she's comfortable with the challenge."

"She'll probably love every minute. Gosh I'm proud

of her."

Kane felt deeply possessive of the little girl. "Me, too."

Harper climbed up the steps onto the deck and then hopped up and down. "I'm so happy. Thank you, Kane. I'll practice like crazy."

"Little ears." Maggie wagged her head.

Kane grinned enjoying every minute in Maggie's and Harper's company. "Are you two up for a beach walk?"

Maggie checked her watch. "I'd love to go for a walk if we can head in the direction of the inn. I'm interviewing Carol Fiore in a half hour."

"Fine with me," he said.

She rose from her seat as Harper turned tail, hopped down onto the sand, and sprinted towards the water's edge. Kane couldn't keep his eyes off Maggie. The ocean breeze had loosened tendrils from her bun that framed her face softly golden. Her eyes were the prettiest shade of green blue, mirroring the sun kissed aqua sea. She wore black shorts cut long enough to be demure and short enough to showcase long shapely legs. Her vee-necked snow-white T-shirt was slightly sheer and clingy in the wind accentuating her lovely figure. Much as he enjoyed Harper's company, he wished that he was alone with Maggie in that instant. Inside. Near a sofa. Or better yet, a bed.

He pushed back his chair, stood, and clasped her hand over the table. Her skin was silken. Kane fantasized about what it would be like to explore all her softness. For now, a handhold would have to suffice.

Kane steered Maggie down on to the sand and followed lazily behind Harper. In the distance he caught sight of four figures splashing in the shallows. The sun haloed their heads glinting reddish orange.

Like Kane, Harper had no trouble identifying his cousins. "There's Miss Skye and the three little Esses."

Did he hear that right? "The little what?"

"Esses. Like the letter S. Serenity, Scarlet, and Spring. Three. Get it?"

Maggie shot him a sidelong glance. "Did you think of that yourself?"

"Uh uh. Miss Skye calls them that. A lot."

Kane and Maggie burst out laughing.

"I'll bet she does," Kane said.

"Can I run ahead?" Harper asked.

"Yes," Maggie said. "We'll be right behind you."

Alone with her, Kane debated pulling Maggie into an embrace or scooping her up, rushing into the water and ravishing her—or better yet, reversing back to the seclusion of his house. No time and not the place.

"So..." he said. "Tell me about your article so far."

"I haven't put all the pieces together yet, but, wow, is this place intriguing. Have you read about the legend of the Inn of the Three Butterflies?"

Don't need to. I grew up in this family. "Can't say that I did."

"Well, it's fascinating. Mysterious. Magical. Babies that can turn into butterflies. All through history back to the early settlers here."

"Wow." *Hang around with the three little Esses long enough and see what happens.* "Are you going to write about that stuff?"

"Oh no. I can't see how that ties in with Christmas other than wishes in a bottle coming true are their own kind of magic."

"Agreed. Do you believe that there's some sort of …magician granting wishes?"

Her melodic laughter flew on the breeze. "Not at all. But the coincidences are mounting up and they sure have my attention."

"I'll say. Do you think you'll get to the bottom of it all?"

"Hmm. I don't see how. People like to believe in magic. Especially at Christmas time. But for sure, I'll keep asking questions."

"Harper told me she's excited about making her own wish in a bottle."

"I know. I hope it's not for a puppy because I'd be astounded if that wish came true. This year I have no intention of buying her one, so the wish genie would have to conjure a dog out of thin air."

"You're safe. Remember she told me that a puppy is her number two wish? She wouldn't tell me number one, because as we all should know, telling someone your wish automatically nullifies it."

"Knew that."

"Of course, you did. You're a mom. Mom knows everything." He gave her a crooked smile.

"Until she turns twelve or so. Then I won't know anything at all." She gifted him a wide grin lighting her lovely face.

He couldn't resist stealing a kiss before they caught up with Harper.

Chapter 9

Three ginger-haired heads rose from digging in the sand as Kane and Maggie approached the toddlers. They squealed one loud screech, dropped their pails and shovels, and ran toward him. Kane squatted open-armed. He embraced the trio in a bear hug and winked up at Maggie.

Kane let them loose and stood up brushing sand off his arms. "Nice castle," he said.

"Thank you," Spring, Serenity and Scarlet sang out in unison. They spun around and lumbered back to Harper and the sandcastle in progress.

Kane waved to Skye standing at the water's edge as if guarding the ocean—he assumed to prevent the little terrors from making a run for the waves.

"Hey Skye," he said. "Can Harper keep playing with the girls a bit longer while Maggie and I walk the beach some more?"

"Sure. No problem."

"Thanks. We won't be long. I have an interview in a little while," Maggie added.

"No hurry. Harper's a great helper."

Harper beamed at Skye's compliment.

"Come on, Maggie." Kane grabbed Maggie's hand and tugged her gently along. "I want to show you something special."

She kept her soft hand curled in his. A sense of

rightness and completion swept over Kane. The woman melted his heart and played endlessly on his mind. One minute he reminded himself that he knew almost nothing about her and the next it seemed that she had always occupied the center of his life. Even Harper had captured his heart. He couldn't get enough of mother and daughter.

"Here we are." He halted in the middle of the beach.

Maggie slowly pirouetted in place knitting her brow. "I don't get it."

"You will." He pointed to a salt-bleached bench perched atop a high dune. "Let's sit for a bit."

He slogged through the sand with Maggie in tow and then plopped down on the bench patting the seat next to him.

She sat down and nestled close to his side. He hung his arm behind her, and she tilted her head to rest against his shoulder.

Kane savored her nearness. "Let me tell you a story," he said. "This bench was built by a man named Ed Kelly who used to live near the inn. Aunt Kay and Uncle Mike knew him well. When his wife Edith started to lose her memory due to Alzheimer's, he built this bench and placed it to overlook her favorite stretch of beach. Every afternoon Ed lovingly brought Edith here. Together they watched the pelicans and seagulls, the ebb and flow of the waves and sighted dolphins. For a few hours every day Edith remembered her devoted husband and they talked and talked. When Ed brought Edith home each time, she slipped away again with no memory of Ed or their life together."

Maggie's jade eyes welled. "Oh no, Kane. That is so sad."

He thumbed away a teardrop spilling down her soft cheek. Guilt stabbed at making her cry. "Aw, don't, Maggie. It is sad. But I think it's beautiful and sort of magical that on this bench despite her grave illness, Edith remembered the love of her life. I want bench love in my life."

She straightened in her seat and regarded him wide-eyed. "Bench love? Wait a minute. Clayton Howard sings a country song called "Bench Love." It's beautiful. Did you write it?"

"I did."

"That's so strange. I interviewed Clayton for *In the Know* and he insinuated the song was his."

Kane snorted. "I'm not surprised. Honestly, the guy is a real jerk. Funny, if he wrote it, why did I receive a Grammy for writing it? I had the condo in LA that I purchased with the royalties to prove it."

"I didn't really care for him when I met him."

"Yeah, he's abrasive and hard to please, but I'm grateful to him. I was an unknown, and he took a chance recording my song." He drew her nearer to him. "When I accepted my Grammy, I thanked Ed Kelly."

"Is Ed still alive?"

"No. But before he passed a few years ago, he still came every day to sit on the bench after Edith died. Towards the end when he needed assistance to walk, Aunt Kay or Uncle Mike would take turns bringing him here. Aunt Kay takes care of the bench now."

He kissed her crown as she nestled her head against his shoulder again. "Tell me more about Maggie Larsen."

"Anything specific you'd like to know?"

"Anything. Everything."

"I'm pretty boring. My job and Harper—that about sums it up."

"I'm sure there's more to such an alluring woman. Dark secrets? Mysterious past? Men vying for your affection?"

"No," she said on a laugh. "But thanks for calling me alluring."

"You certainly are that." Kane took his phone out of his pocket. "I have an idea." He fiddled with his phone and then said, "Have you ever played never have I ever?"

"I seem to answer every one of your questions with a no. Why?"

Kane pointed to his phone. "Would you believe google results for the game are two hundred and fifty questions? Want to play?"

"Why not?"

"Number one on the list: Never have I ever faked sick to get out of work."

"Who hasn't?" Maggie said.

He nodded. "Me, too. Especially when I was waiting tables way back when. Next is, Gone skinny dipping."

"Again, who hasn't?"

He grinned. "Would like to revisit that one with you."

She tapped him playfully on the side of his arm. "Keep reading."

"Been arrested?"

"Of course not," she said.

Kane moved on. "How about…"

"Wait a minute," she interjected. "Have you been arrested?"

"Kind of goes with the skinny-dipping question. Does being stuffed into the back of a police car after skinny dipping in a public fountain count as being arrested?"

She arched her brows. "Are you serious? Wow. Did you go to jail?"

"No. The cops were used to the football team getting drunk and acting like idiots. They took me back to the dorm and told me to sleep it off. Typical college stuff."

Maggie burst out laughing delighting Kane. "Your college experience and mine were very different. What time is it, Kane?"

"Ten to two."

"I've got to run. Literally. I have an interview appointment in ten minutes." She rose from the bench.

"How about one more," he said. "Never have I ever dated my daughter's piano teacher."

"Yes, I never. I do find him incredibly hot, though, considering."

Kane knit his brow. "Considering, what?"

"Considering he's seventy-five years old. Don't get me wrong. I like older men, but he has been happily married for fifty-three years. So… I just have to live with what if."

He snorted a laugh. "You're a brat. Do you know that?"

Fake innocence shone in her wide-eyed expression. "I don't know what you mean. I was just answering honestly."

"Maybe I can help you get over him. Would you like to go to dinner tonight?"

"I would love to, but I can't leave Harper alone."

"I'm pretty sure Aunt Kay or Skye would babysit. Can I ask them?"

"That sounds just perfect." She pecked a kiss on his

lips.

"I'll text you a time if I can arrange it." He wanted much more than a peck on the lips, but Harper was racing toward them, her long hair flying in the wind.

Panting, she thrust her fist under Maggie's nose and then opened her hand revealing a tiny, perfect sand dollar. "Look what I found!"

"A treasure," Kane said. "I've never found one myself. Fun fact—in New Zealand they're called sea cookies."

"That is so funny. Skye said I can keep it," Harper said.

"Of course, you can. Let's take it back to the inn. I have work," Maggie said.

Maggie and Harper walked away from him hand in hand, their laughter floating on the breeze. A weird yearning overtook him watching them leave. He longed for them to come back.

****

Maggie had just enough time to run a brush through her hair and grab her notebook before her meeting. She rushed down to the kitchen after situating Harper in their room with a coloring book and crayons.

Carol was seated at the table with a mug of tea in front of her dressed in a gaily colored print blouse and black slacks. Her short, pixie-cut blonde hair was perfectly styled. She wore just enough makeup to give the impression that she wore no makeup, understated and casual elegant.

"Hi," Maggie said. She helped herself to a cup of coffee before taking a seat opposite Carol. "I hope I haven't kept you waiting."

"I just sat down." Carol stared fixedly into her cup

of tea.

"Is this a bad time for you? You seem uncomfortable."

"I kind of am. Full disclosure: I asked Kay if she really wanted me to expose my experience with my wish in a bottle. In the past I had the feeling that Kay wanted to keep our stories secret."

Maggie frowned. "Kay hasn't been secretive with me at all."

"Maybe secret is not the right word. I think private is a better word."

"Kay gave me her blessing to do what I do. But, of course speaking with me is voluntary. I would never want to make you feel uncomfortable."

"I'm sorry. I think we got off on the wrong foot." Carol held out her hand smiling. "Hi, my name is Carol, nice to meet you," she said with a soft southern drawl.

Maggie gave her hand a shake. "A pleasure. Feel free to tell me if you'd rather not answer any question. May we start?"

Carol nodded.

"Were you staying at the inn on Christmas Day when Julie Donovan was here five years ago?"

"No, I wasn't."

"How did you hear about Julie?"

"I never heard of Julie until I came here four years ago. Bob, my husband, gave me the trip for Christmas. Bob knows how much I love the ocean and we have always wanted to come to the Outer Banks. I was depressed and he was hoping to cheer me up. It's a long story, but my daughter and I were estranged for years after my divorce. Her father and I divorced when she was eighteen, a freshman in college. She was always a

Daddy's girl and she wanted nothing to do with me after the divorce was final.

"I missed her terribly, especially during the holidays. No matter what I did—sent texts, emails, gifts for special occasions, of course Christmas gifts, she refused to acknowledge me, even banning me from her college graduation. Christmas Eve night Bob fell asleep early. I couldn't sleep. I couldn't stop thinking about the bottle that was on the desk when we checked in. So, I took some stationery and a pen along with the bottle and went outside on the deck. I shone my phone's flashlight on the paper and just sat there with the pen in my hand. For the longest time I didn't know what to write. Then an amazing peace filled me. I simply wished that my girl would come back to me in her own time. I stuffed the paper in the bottle and threw it in the ocean." Tears streamed down Carol's face.

Maggie's eyes filled with tears. She reached across the table and held Carol's hand.

"Sorry." Carol dabbed her eyes with a napkin.

"Don't be. If you want to take a break or stop, we can."

Carol smiled. "We can't stop now. I'm just getting to the good part."

She took a deep breath. "Honestly with Christmas the next day I forgot about the bottle. We were leaving the day after Christmas very early in the morning. I just had to walk the beach one more time before we went home, so I got up before dawn on Christmas Day and walked down to the shoreline. I found a corked bottle, maybe my bottle, in the sand. I was disappointed that I hadn't apparently tossed it hard enough to send it out to sea. I picked it up and discovered that it was empty, although it was corked. I figured it wasn't mine after all but decided to keep it as a pretty souvenir.

"I finished my walk and headed back to the inn ready to devour my breakfast and find some joy celebrating the holiday with my darling second husband in this lovely place.

"When I walked into the kitchen, Bob greeted me smiling like crazy. He drew me towards the parlor and when we reached the doorway, he stepped aside. My daughter sat on the couch beaming at me. I was stupefied and speechless, but I opened my arms to her, and she ran into my embrace.

"When I finally found my tongue and asked how, why, she told me that my son had called her on Christmas Eve to wish her Merry Christmas and something compelled her to ask my whereabouts. She told me she was sorry for abandoning me and knew then that she could love her dad *and* her mom even though they weren't together." Carol took a ragged breath. "She told me she missed me. This is the story of my Christmas wish in a bottle."

"You believe you wished your daughter back into your life?" Maggie couldn't hide her skeptical tone.

"I do. But I see that you don't believe it at all. That's the reason I'm not comfortable talking about this with you. And neither are any of the other guests, Maggie. I'm surprised that Kay has even sanctioned publicity about this."

Given this farfetched thinking, Maggie was surprised, too. "I've agreed with Kay's request to approve my article before I submit it to my editor. If she doesn't like it, I will either revise it to her satisfaction or scrap it completely. You have my word."

Carol gave Maggie a nod as she rose from her seat.

Maggie stood up and rounded the table to give Carol a hug, pleased that she hugged her back. "I'm thrilled that you're reconciled with your daughter, and I truly appreciate your entrusting your story to me."

"Thanks, Maggie. I'm sure I'll see you around."

Maggie's phone vibrated in her pocket. She hoped the text was from Kane.

She opened the message app and wasn't disappointed. His message confirmed his Aunt Kay's eager agreement to watch Harper while he took her out that evening. He signed off, *Can't wait.*

A date! With a man like Kane who, she imagined, could date any woman he wanted.

And he wants me. She could hardly contain her excitement. Gathering up her notes she hurried to her room to shower, do her hair, and pick out something special to wear. When was the last time that she went on a date? Not since before she was pregnant with Harper, for sure—so long ago, she couldn't remember precisely.

She glanced at his text again. *Oh, Kane. I can't wait either.*

Chapter 10

"You look perfect," Kane's eyes shone in the parlor's lamplight.

His tousled raven hair curled at the ends, fringing the collar of his immaculate white shirt. He wore a form-fitting powder blue sport coat that deepened the sapphire color of his eyes and tailored jeans. The man looked magazine spread worthy.

Meeting a handsome celebrity there in a largely unpopulated seasonal town was the last thing that Maggie had anticipated, no less that the celebrity would want to…

Exactly what Kane wanted with Maggie remained unclear to her. Maybe she was out of practice in the dating game, or maybe Kane's playboy reputation had her reluctant to give too much import to what was going on with them.

Maggie had enormous research capability at her disposal. She had unrestricted access to the magazine's network of databases which she used routinely to corroborate facts for publication. Having never used the research network for personal reasons, Maggie had felt almost criminal doing background checking on Kane and scrutinizing media mentions of him. She had discovered nothing disturbing about him—except for the parade of gorgeous, in-the-news women linked to him in the past.

She had no delusions that she could compete with

the supermodels, actresses and megastar singers he had purportedly dated. So why was he standing there calling her perfect? Well, she had taken pains to look her best that evening wearing the only dress she had packed—a black velvet midi length hem with a scooped neck and three-quarter length sleeves that had always garnered compliments in the past. A vintage Hattie Carnegie Christmas tree brooch was clasped on the dress over her left collarbone, and she wore dainty black velvet flats, each adorned with a small red satin bow, for festive holiday touches.

He arched one eyebrow and took a couple of steps towards her. "Maggie are you okay?" he said snapping her out of her reverie.

"Uh yes," she stammered wagging her head to banish her lapse in confidence. "Thank you. You look perfect yourself."

"And thank *you*. I have to look my best if I want to deserve you on my arm. Do you have a sweater or jacket to wear later? We'll be outside and it might get chilly."

Drifting over to the seating arrangement, Maggie picked up the wrap she had placed over the back of the sofa. "All set."

He crooked an elbow. "Shall we?"

Maggie wrapped her fingers around his bicep. He briefly covered her hand with his large, warm hand sending tingles up her arm, and then led her outside to his car: a fire engine red Italian-made convertible, low to the ground with feline headlights and an iconic hood ornament.

If she hadn't felt cowed by Kane's celebrity before, she did then, seated in his uber-hot car. She wanted to exclaim, "Wow!" But she held her tongue as if she rode in sports cars with gorgeous men routinely.

He pulled out onto the beach road and worked the gear shift vamping up the engine from housecat purring into a leonine roar. In her head Maggie exclaimed, "Whee!"

"Where are we going?" she said.

"First, dinner at my favorite restaurant on the Banks. Do you like seafood?"

"Love it."

"Then you'll love the menu. After dinner I thought we'd visit the Elizabethan Gardens. Their holiday display gets better every year."

She settled in the contoured seat thrilled at the evening ahead.

Kane was right. The menu in the quaint, waterfront restaurant was so extensive, she had trouble deciding which dish she most wanted to sample. And Kane was no help when she asked him for a recommendation. He vowed that she couldn't go wrong no matter what she chose cautioning her not to let the downhome southern dishes fool her. The chef delivered world class cuisine and the freshest seafood around.

Putting her fork down when she couldn't eat another bite, she said, "That was the most delicious sword fish I have ever eaten. Thank you, Kane."

"You're very welcome." His smile and the warmth that he projected gazing deeply into her eyes across the candlelit table had her beaming back at him.

He set his forearms flat on the table extending his upturned palms across to her. She placed her hands in his, the most natural, intimate gesture as if they belonged connected—had always belonged connected. Kane might not have meant to stir passion in her with such an innocent handhold, but Maggie experienced a floaty sensuality with his touch as if he were hers and she, his.

They sat like that surrounded by fairy lights on the outside patio, warmed beneath the gas heater until a waiter asked if they wanted to order dessert.

"I'm pretty full. Should we?" She retracted her hands and straightened in her chair.

"No, thank you, just the check," he directed the waiter.

"There will be plenty of dessert items at the Gardens if you want something sweet later," Kane said.

Maggie gazed out the window of his car as they zoomed across the bridge over Roanoke Sound that connected Nags Head and Roanoke Island. Christmas lights decorating the homes along the shoreline of the island town of Manteo glimmered reflecting blurry starlight on the surface of the Sound's inky waters.

Kane switched on the radio filling the cabin with Gene Autry's smooth voice crooning "Frosty The Snowman." The prospect of snow seemed impossible on that sixty-degree evening making Maggie long for a white Christmas Chicago-style. But after they had parked the car, took a bag of groceries from the trunk, and entered the Elizabethan Gardens into a wonderland of lighted holiday displays, her homesickness was replaced by childlike nostalgia.

"Wow, look at all the people." She shuffled on a walking path after Kane had handed over the groceries at the gift shop counter.

"It's Virginia Dare night when entrance is free with a donation to the local food pantry."

"That's wonderful."

The trunks and branches of towering oak trees were

wrapped tightly with fairy lights. Fires blazed along the walkways and volunteers dressed in Elizabethan garb handed out marshmallows for roasting and wet wipes for sticky fingers. A giant snowman bench was illuminated all around with snowflakes. Shrubs were encrusted with tiny lights, some blinking on and off, others twinkling red, green, and white. Luminescent stars hung in the trees; flower beds were a sea of lights; a sunken garden was a pool of radiance; walking paths were rimmed with stationary lights; multi-color strands ringed fountains; decorated Christmas trees resplendent with lit candles positioned around every corner; and glowing forms of reindeer, snowmen, Queen Elizabeth, and her footman, completed the tableaus.

Maggie gasped in delight at each turn as Kane held her hand and meandered with her along the Garden's paver stone paths. They entered a clearing where choir-robed children clustered on a platform. Two identical keyboards on stands with small benches tucked underneath stood in front of the platform. A crowd of people milled around in a tight group in front of the choir.

Kane steered Maggie through the throng smiling and uttering, excuse us, until they reached the front of the pack.

"Hey guys," Kane called out.

The kids waved and chattered and yelled hello to Mister Kane. He kissed Maggie's hand. "I have a little job to do. Hope you like it," he said.

He sat down on one of the piano benches and then gave a head nod to his right. Maggie's jaw dropped when Harper emerged from behind a tree trunk, beamed at her and then sat at the keyboard next to Kane. Her daughter wore a red velvet dress with matching Mary Jane shoes that Maggie had never seen before. Her hair was a riot of raven curls clipped away from her face with tiny, crystal, bow-shaped barrettes.

A gentle touch on her shoulder had Maggie spinning around.

"Hi, Maggie," Kay grinned at her. "Do you like the surprise Kane and Harper cooked up for you?"

"My gosh, I'm stunned. Are they going to play together?"

"You bet," Mike said. "This is just a brief sampling of the Christmas Eve concert according to Kane."

"Where did Harper get the dress?"

Kay's eyes gleamed. "Skye and I might have had something to do with that. Do you like it?"

"She looks beautiful. How much do I owe you?"

"Oh," Kay waved a hand in dismissal. "Consider it an early Christmas present."

Maggie looked over her shoulder watching Kane quiet the kids down as Kay and Mike moved to stand at her side. She faced forward. He turned his attention to Harper. She poised on the edge of the bench, her eyes glued to Kane. He said something softly to her. Both Harper and Kane wore such loving expressions focused on each other that Maggie's heart swelled. Was it possible that he loved her girl and Harper loved him back?

She gave her head a quick shake instinctively rejecting the notion as too good to be true. Still her heart beat a little faster at the clear adoration Harper exuded in Kane's thrall.

Kane tapped the microphone three amplified knocks and the crowd quieted. "Good evening, folks. Most of you know me, but just in case, I'm Kane Martin. And this beautiful young lady at the keyboard is Harper Larsen, a talented musician visiting from Chicago at The Inn Of The Three Butterflies."

His velvety baritone sparked a lovely burst of possession in Maggie. Her daughter, her man.

Applause sounded and Harper's cheeks flamed crimson spurring a flood of mama bear protectiveness in Maggie. Harper had zero performance experience except for small recitals arranged by her piano teachers. She prayed Kane knew what he was doing spotlighting her little girl.

"Ladies and gentlemen, I proudly present the OBX Youth Chorus and The Seven Song Christmas Mashup," Kane announced.

He raised his hand and paused waiting for all eyes to train on him. He signaled, begin, with an exaggerated nod of his head and the drop of his hand. Harper took the lead accompanying the first song in the medley, "Deck The Halls." Kane conducted and then played the bass clef notes while Harper played the treble clef part for "Jingle Bells." Then Harper and Kane played each of the two melodies at the same time while the chorus divided in half singing both songs mashed together in four-part harmonies with fugue runs and madrigal-like flourishes. The piano music soared as both Harper and Kane played "Angels We Have Heard On High" an octave apart. The chorus harmonized during the refrain beautifully.

Maggie burst with pride listening to Harper's flawless playing and witnessing her poised concentration in front of so many people. Kane seemed to treat Harper and the young choir members respectfully without a shred of condescension. Each snippet of Christmas song favorites had Kane and Harper either dueling or duetting and the chorus following suit. The concert finished with a rousing, and loud, four stanzas of "We Wish You A Merry Christmas."

If the crowd weren't already standing at the open-air performance, Maggie was certain that their thunderous ovation would have propelled them to their feet. Kane remained seated at the keyboard signaling Harper to stand facing the audience and take a bow. Clapping continued as the kids in the chorus bowed over and over grinning widely.

"Thank you, thank you," Kane's voice boomed through the mic. "We hope to see you at the Village Christmas Eve Concert. Tickets are available at local merchants and online at the Chamber of Commerce website. Thank you for supporting the Roanoke Food Pantry tonight. Merry Christmas."

Maggie rushed toward Harper and Kane as if floating in a dream. Could the evening have been more perfect? She doubted it. Kane had played her heartstrings as expertly as he played the piano. The best part was that he seemed as genuinely delighted in Harper's company as he did in Maggie's. Could Kane be more perfect for her? She doubted that, too.

She threw her arms around Harper, gushing praise.

"Thanks, Mommy. It was fun."

No grandstanding or bragging from her girl. Maggie thought she'd explode with pride.

Kane's grin melted Maggie's heart. He took her hand, kissed it softly and then turned toward Harper. "You did great, kiddo. Before we leave, I think we have plenty of time for some roasted marshmallows and a visit to Father Christmas over there. What do you think?"

"Oh yes. Can I, Mommy?"

"Of course," Maggie said.

"You and Kane feel free to wander," Kay interjected. "Mike and I want to play some with Harper. I promise I'll have her back to the inn in an hour or so. If it's okay to stay up past her bedtime, that is."

"It is. She can sleep as late as she wants tomorrow," Maggie said triggering Harper to jump up and down.

Maggie gave Harper a hug and kissed her on her shampoo fragrant crown. "See you later, sweetie."

Harper clasped Kay's hand. "Bye, Mommy."

Kane circled his arm around Maggie's shoulders. "Want some marshmallows?"

"Nah. How about another ride in your awesome car?"

"You got it. Let's go."

Maggie couldn't stop smiling as they walked towards the parking lot beneath twinkling boughs in the magical garden.

Chapter 11

Kane had left early the morning after their magical date for a recording session of the soundtrack he had composed for a film. Three days later Maggie might have dreamed the wonderful visit to Elizabethan Gardens if it weren't for the red velvet dress hung in Harper's closet. *The Outer Banks Voice* had published a front page spread of the festivities. A photo of Harper and Kane smiling at each other headed the article.

Maggie had scrounged two more copies of the issue at Harper's request so that she could cut out the pictures for framing: one for Harper to keep and one for her to give to her grandparents as a belated Christmas gift.

Although she had kept busy interviewing guests, working on her article's preliminary draft, and enjoying free time with her daughter, Maggie had repeatedly checked her phone for word from Kane like a teenager waiting for an invitation to the prom. Had she imagined the powerful connection building between her and Kane? Maybe she was foolish to believe that a gorgeous man who had women drooling over him was interested in a relationship with a simple, single mom like her—or interested in any relationship. Did he want commitment…marriage…a family—especially a built-in one with her? No idea.

She checked the phone again as soon as she awoke and pursed her lips, disappointed again. No word from him yet. Rubbing her eyes, she sat up, leaned her back against the headboard and glanced over at Harper. The sight of her beautiful daughter in innocent slumber in the bed next to hers made her heart skip. Not a day went by that Maggie didn't take a moment to thank God for the gift of Harper.

As if feeling her mother's gaze on her, Harper stretched and opened her eyes.

"Good morning, sunshine," Maggie said.

"Morning, Mommy." She hopped out of bed apparently ready for action. "Can I please go practice the piano today?"

Maggie hesitated. Kane had insisted that Harper could use his music room anytime in his absence. But she had avoided going to Kane's empty house. Instead, she had spent her free time playing with Harper on the beach and taking day trips. But Harper missed her music and Maggie wasn't sure when Kane would return. She decided she'd feel selfish if she refused.

"Yes," Maggie said. "Let's take a walk on the beach, eat breakfast and then we can go to Kane's. How does that sound?"

****

Harper picked up tiny shells while Maggie reveled in the warm sunshine and watched the dolphins play in the waves on a beach walk. Despite her enjoyment of the moment, Maggie wished Kane was walking by her side.

"I wish Mister Kane was here with us," Harper said.

My little mind reader. Kane had so rapidly become a part of their lives that it frightened Maggie. She didn't have much time left on her working vacation and they would resume their normal life in Chicago. Without Kane? He *had* mentioned his Chicago residence several times hinting at a future for them. Was she wrong to let Harper get close to Kane knowing they would have to leave soon?

She gave her head a shake dispelling negative thinking. For once in her life, she would fully enjoy the moment and not worry about what would or wouldn't happen. Her spirits raised, she clasped Harper's hand and skipped along the water's edge back to the inn where Kay's famous chocolate chip pancakes called to them.

After stuffing herself with a delicious breakfast, Maggie decided to walk off some calories. The weather was perfect, and she couldn't get enough beach time away from Chicago winter.

Refreshed by the mild exertion and the natural beauty outdoors, Maggie and Harper arrived at Kane's house. She smiled as she punched in his non-secure, security code and nearly tripped over a leather satchel on the floor in the hallway when she stepped away from the security panel on the wall.

Was Kane back? Her mood shot from good to great at the prospect.

"Kane!" she called out. "Are you home?"

No response.

She followed Harper to the piano, got her situated, and paced down the hallway to Kane's room. The door was ajar, and the bed was neatly made. Disappointed, she returned to the music room, snuggled into the comfy couch cushions, and opened her book. She closed her eyes and listened to the beautiful music Harper created.

The scent of his cologne filled her senses before she felt the soft touch of his lips on hers. The kiss intensified and Maggie was lost. She threaded her fingers through his hair and pulled his head closer.

But then…Kane shook her arm.

She blinked open her eyes encountering Harper's face inches from hers.

"You fell asleep. You must have been dreaming. You said, 'Kane, more'."

Maggie sat up straight, blushing to the roots of her hair. The dream felt so real. "Oh…" she scrambled for a reasonable explanation for her five-year-old. "I was dreaming of those delicious chocolate chip pancakes. And in my dream Kane was having breakfast with us and I asked him for more."

"That's cool." Harper handed Maggie her music folio. "I'm done practicing. Can we walk back on the beach like before?"

"Sure." Maggie shoved her unread book and Harper's things in the backpack and then led the way outside.

Mid-way back to the inn, low hanging clouds turned charcoal gray and the heavens opened drenching Harper and Maggie to the skin. Giggling, they clomped up the stairs leading off the beach and stood on the deck dripping wet.

Kay ran outside with plush beach towels for them and joined in their laughter. "Thank goodness it's warm here today." She dried Harper's sopping wet hair.

"I bet we'd have frostbite if we were home," Harper dramatized.

"Oh look!" She pointed to the sky over the ocean as the sun poked through the clouds. "Make a wish, Mommy."

A beautiful rainbow arced over the undulating silver-colored waves. The trio stood in place and closed their eyes following Harper's suggestion. After she made a wish having to do with Kane and Chicago, Maggie took her phone out of the zipper pouch on the side of the backpack and took a picture of Harper with the rainbow overhead.

Maggie bent her head over her phone to message the photo to her parents. She had missed two calls and several texts from an unknown number since she had silenced the phone during Harper's practice session.

She'd check the messages after a hot shower. Maggie slipped the phone back in the backpack and broke into a run towards the patio door.

"Beat you to our room," she challenged Harper.

Giggling, Harper dropped her towel and whizzed past Maggie.

Since she won the race, Harper had first dibs on the shower. Maggie scooped up Harper's soggy clothes, peeled off her clothes, wrapped herself in a terry cloth robe and then opened her door to take the wet things downstairs to the drier. In the hall Kay greeted her toting a plastic laundry basket relieving Maggie of her dripping bundle.

"Thanks, Kay."

Seated on her bed waiting for her turn in the bathroom, Maggie checked her voicemail and text messages. The unknown calls and texts were from Kane. He'd forgotten the bag that Maggie had seen in the hallway at his house. It contained his phone and computer. He apologized for not getting in touch sooner, but his work had prevented him from buying a disposable phone until that day.

"I'll be home tomorrow morning," he had recorded in voicemail. "I hope you and Harper are free to spend the afternoon with me. I can't wait to see you."

Maggie couldn't stop smiling having received her "prom invitation." She listened to the message three times before it was her turn to take a shower.

****

Maggie heard Kane burst out laughing as she descended the back stairs leading to the kitchen. She paused at the bottom of the staircase and listened to Harper's high-pitched laughter and the cheerful banter between her and Kane.

She hurried into the kitchen and Kane turned his attention to her.

He gazed at her, his eyes shining, and sauntered toward her open-armed. It felt so right to walk straight into his arms.

His hug warmed her and sent a zing of happiness through her.

"It is so good to see you." He gave her a squeeze and then took a step away from her.

"You can help settle an argument I'm having with this little one." He tugged on Harper's ponytail.

Kay huffed a laugh as she took another batch of cupcakes out of the oven. Kane pointed to two cupcakes out of several dozen lining the kitchen table. One was glazed precisely with chocolate icing dusted evenly with red and green sprinkles. Icing dripped unevenly down the sides of the second cupcake and a heap of sprinkles piled on top.

"Which one would you pick?" he said.

"Hmm." Maggie cupped her chin faced with a Rockefeller Center versus Charlie Brown tree decision.

And surely, she faced a Harper versus Kane decision in picking a winner. Harper was usually neat, so Maggie took a chance and chose the prettier cupcake.

"You're kidding me! Anyone would pick the one with the most icing and sprinkles." Kane winked at Maggie.

He seized his Charlie Brown cupcake and aggressively bit into it. Sprinkles snowed on the tabletop and floor. Kane wore a chocolate icing mustache.

Impulsively, Maggie traced Kane's mouth with her index finger, swiped off icing and then put her finger in her mouth.

His eyes locked on hers as he slowly wiped off the rest of the icing with a napkin.

"Harper, honey. Come help me test these cupcakes," Kay said reading the room.

"Never have I ever seen anything more erotic," he whispered in Maggie's ear raising goosebumps on Maggie's arms and triggering a flash of heat through her system. She didn't have to glance in a mirror to know that her cheeks had blushed scarlet.

She bustled over to the sink to wet a paper towel to clean up the mess on the floor, mostly for something to do with her hands.

Kay shooed her away. "I'll take care of that, Maggie. Why don't you three eat your snack out on the deck?"

"Okay, thanks."

Kay loaded a tray with two mugs of coffee, a glass of milk and three cupcakes and then handed it to Kane. She preceded him and opened the sliding glass door.

As Harper passed in front of her, Kay said, "Thank you for your help today, honey. I'll see you at the airport later."

"The airport?" Maggie said pulling a chair over to the table.

"Oh Mommy, wait 'til you hear. Kane told me all about the candy bomber."

"What's the candy bomber, Kane?" Maggie said.

"It all started with the Berlin Airlift and Colonel Gail Halvorsen," he said. "During World War II the people of West Berlin were completely isolated from western Europe. Halvorsen and his fellow British airmen along with American pilots flew up to three times a day dropping supplies to keep the city alive. When Halvorsen saw children lining up below air drops, he decided to tie up his own rations of chocolate bars into handkerchief-parachutes. The next time he flew to West Berlin he dropped the candy bombs to the children. The kids went crazy with delight. His men joined in and donated their rations, too. When a German journalist wrote about the drop, news spread to the United States informing The Hershey Company of the extraordinary missions. The company donated candy for the special bombs. In the end they dropped more than three tons of candy over Berlin."

"What a wonderful story. But what does this have to do with Kay's comment about the airport?" Maggie said.

"This is the best part," Harper said.

"When a woman named Karin Edmond, who had experienced the drops as a child in Berlin and lives in Manteo now, heard the C54 Spirit of Freedom, a replica of the plane that Halvorsen piloted, was at Dare County Regional Airport in Manteo, she had to go see it. She never forgot the candy bombs.

"She helped raise funds to sponsor an annual candy drop at the airport during the holiday season. Colonel Halvorsen flew over the airport for twenty-three years in a row. Sadly, he passed away last year. Karin, who had become his close friend, promised him the last time she talked with him right before he died, that she would keep the wonder of the reenactment going for the children. The candy bomber will fly over the airport today. One Christmas when we were visiting, Uncle Mike took Ty and me to meet Colonel Halvorsen. I will never forget that day," Kane said.

"That is why I was helping Miss Kay make the cupcakes." Harper took another bite. "She will bring them to the airport. Please can we go?" Harper said with her mouth full.

"I wouldn't miss it for the world," Maggie said already thinking about documenting the joyful experience in her article.

They finished their treats gazing out at the ocean as Harper fairly vibrated with excitement.

Kane gave a nod toward her daughter, his eyes twinkling. "I think we better head out before she explodes. We can transport some of the cupcakes for Aunt Kay."

Harper launched out of her seat, scooped up their empty plates and zipped inside.

"She's pretty excited," Kane remarked.

Maggie snorted a laugh. "Ya think?"

****

Harper, Maggie, and Kane each carried a tray of cupcakes towards the tables set up under a tent at the airfield. People milled around and children arched their necks scanning the cloudless skies for the plane. Kane introduced Maggie and Harper to Karin Edmond. Harper was star struck and couldn't find her words at first. In parting, she managed to say that she would donate her birthday money next year for the candy bomber.

Maggie overheard Karin thank Kane profusely for

his "amazing donation", but Kane switched the gratitude around and thanked her for all she did to keep this Outer Banks tradition alive.

It was Maggie's turn to be star struck. Once again Kane demonstrated his goodness and Maggie fell harder for this kind, generous man at every turn.

The unmistakable whine of an airplane engine overrode the sound of the crowd's conversations and a hush fell over the gathering. Chills raced over Maggie's arms when the plane came into view.

Volunteers including Kay and Skye, herded the kids into an area marked off with a painted red bullseye. Parents were directed to stand on the perimeter with cameras at the ready. The majestic four-prop plane flew overhead, and a few tiny parachutes floated downward.

Maggie's heart swelled at the cheerful atmosphere. The children didn't push or shove or try to selfishly grab candy. The plane made a return pass overhead releasing hundreds of candy bombs—a horde of snow-white parcels raining down in the azure sky. With outstretched arms, the kids caught the flying treats, sharing with each other so that not a single child was left without candy.

Harper carried her parachute as if it were precious gold walking to Kane's car.

"I can't wait to show Grandpa. He told me that his dad was in the war, and he jumped out of planes with a parachute. Wow, right?" She clicked her seatbelt in place in the back seat.

"That is a definite wow." Kane brought Maggie's hand to his lips and kissed her knuckles one at time.

"Yes, definitely a wow," she whispered, gazing into his eyes.

Chapter 12

Kane scratched his head, assessing the ragtag procession over the picturesque footbridge. In his mind's eye the children's choir, who currently shuffled or dragged or clomped their feet, would float like angels over the bridge and onto the sprawling lawn fronting the magnificent historic mansion on the night of the concert. Admittedly in broad daylight without candles in their hands or the Christmas lights on the estate blazing, it was challenging to inspire hushed seriousness during rehearsal. The only kid who met with Kane's perfectionist standards was Harper. Her poise never failed to amaze him.

Should he single her out to model behavior for the rest of the kids? Although he was far from an expert on children, even he knew that was a bad idea. Tempting, though. He held his irritation in check as the choir straggled to a halt in front of him. Times like those he wanted to strangle his family for roping him in to directing the concert. He was used to working with professional musicians—colleagues. How had he wound up virtually babysitting?

"So. How do you think that went?" He ping-ponged his head from side-to-side pinning the fresh-faced crew with a scowl. "Anybody?"

A lot of squirming went on, but no one volunteered a response.

"Hmmm." He cupped his chin and cast his eyes downward as if lost in thought. "Hang on," he said in motion toward the three-sided tent where the concert would take place.

He jogged forward, grabbed a candle holder off a long table, reversed and jogged back to the kids.

"Okay," he said. "Harper, can you please play the entrance music for me?"

She knit her brow and pointed to the tent. "Back there?"

"Yes, please."

"But…I don't think I can play hard enough for you to hear me."

"That's all right. We have to use our imaginations. There will be speakers everywhere during the night of the concert. And I'll be playing while you lead the procession, Harper, not you. For now, the choir will hear you from here, I think. That will work for my demonstration. You guys stay here and start singing when she cues you. I want to show you how I'd like you to walk across the bridge.

"Let me get into position first, Kevin," Kane said to the tall twelve-year old with sandy brown hair flopping in his eyes standing at the front of the pack. "When I'm on the other side of the bridge, raise your hand so that Harper knows when to begin."

"Sure thing, Mister K."

Kane spun on his heel and sprinted over the bridge, his thunderous footfalls setting the opposite example for the kids. He turned around and paused for a moment drinking in the beautiful landscape in front of him. The castle-like home painted pale yellow gracefully dominated the grounds. Five redbrick chimney stacks topped the deeply sloping roof above nine dormer windows. Acres of manicured lawn and footpaths lined with shrubs and mature oak trees strung with Christmas lights sprawled at the edge of the Sound's tributary spanned by the antique footbridge in front of him. The snow-white tent erected in the foreground added a note of holiday festivity.

He gave an exaggerated nod. Kevin raised his arm. The choir began singing "Angels We Have Heard On High."

Stepping forward as if marching down a bridal aisle, Kane maintained a reverent posture placing each foot lightly down on the wooden flooring as he crossed the bridge.

When he reached the kids who were singing for all they were worth he said, "Fall in behind me, guys. Let's go take the stage."

Now Kane could hear Harper playing the heck out of the piano. The choir's voices soared at the chorus of the carol, executing the simple harmonies for the lyrics, "Gloria In Excelsis Deo," that he had taught them. As he entered the tent, Kane stepped aside observing the kids file in and mount the risers—surprisingly in a smooth, orderly assembly. Happy that the children took him seriously, he strode forward, sat at the piano opposite Harper, and finished playing the accompaniment with her an octave higher.

When they concluded playing, she lifted her hands gracefully off the keyboard like a pro. She sat ladylike on the bench with her hands folded in her lap, her crystalline blue eyes wide and trained on him.

Kane beamed at her hoping she understood how pleased he was with her conduct without his saying so.

The last thing he wanted was to label her as teacher's pet. Even though she, hands down, was increasingly his pet in so many ways more than her musical talent.

He genuinely enjoyed Harper's company and found himself excited at the prospect of teaching her, treating her to holiday experiences, even just talking with her. Kane loved the way her mind worked. He loved her sweetness, innocence, and just plain goodness. Truthfully, he was falling in love with her almost as much as he'd fallen for Maggie.

Unexpectedly the holiday season had become joyful for Kane because Maggie and Harper had come to the inn. He couldn't remember looking forward to Christmas this much in adulthood. Kane wanted kisses under the mistletoe, cuddling by fires, jaunts to see Christmas lights—even singing Christmas carols, with Maggie. Kane couldn't imagine life without Maggie and Harper.

All those thoughts flew through his head and tangled up in his heart. Normally, he'd direct himself to get a grip, refocus, and concentrate on work which was all that mattered. He could no more give up his work than stop breathing. But unexpectedly, he felt the same way about giving up Maggie.

The program called for the children's choir to perform three songs. Next, the adult choir would sing three songs, also. He and Harper would play his composition afterward, and then the combined choirs would finish the concert singing "Have Yourself A Merry Little Christmas" while leaving the tent in a candlelight procession.

Kane had rehearsed with the adult choir the day before and was satisfied with their readiness to perform. The kids, not so much.

"Okay, guys," he said. "One more time singing "Frosty The Snowman" and then pretend you have candles in your hands, and we'll practice filing out at the end of the concert while you sing the finale song. Sound good?"

Kane and Harper played the accompaniment to Frosty together and then he launched into the intro bars of the processional song.

"Now," he hollered over his playing, "follow Harper and pretend that you're coming in and when you get to the bridge, walk like I showed you."

Harper popped up from her seat, mimed holding her candle in front of her and positioned at the edge of the bottom riser to lead the procession. She set in motion as singing began.

Instead of following her, the little girl in the first position on the riser raised her hand. "Mister K, Mister K," she called out stopping Harper in her tracks.

He cut off playing. Now what? "Yes, Mandy?"

"I don't understand. How do we pretend coming in when we're going out?"

"Uh..." *Wow, kids are literal.* "I mean walk across the bridge slowly and gently. Like I did before."

"Oh. Okay," she agreed.

Kane lifted his hands to the keyboard, but more arms raised and wagged amid a barrage of calling out his name.

"More questions, I see." He pointed to a boy in the front row. "You."

"But how do we hear the music out there?"

He resisted rolling his eyes. "You probably won't. Just keep singing and make your own music."

"What if it rains Christmas Eve?" came another.

"Good question. It's not predicted, but if it does, we can hold the concert inside the mansion and we can walk down the main staircase holding our candles."

"What if there's a nor'easter? Or a hurricane?" came another.

Kane chuckled. "Same answer for nor'easter. I'm pretty sure that we don't have to worry about a hurricane. Next?"

"What if it snows?"

"Wow, that would be something," Kane said. "I'd say if it snows, if it's not a blizzard or anything, we can still walk over the bridge and hold the concert here. Maybe put on some boots. There are plenty of space heaters in the tent."

He positioned his hands over the keyboard again, but another "Mister K" rang out drawing his reluctant attention. "Yes, Gail?"

"Where do we go when we walk out if we do the concert inside the house?"

"Right up those stairs you came down at the beginning." Kane wanted nothing more at that point than to finally finish the rehearsal.

"Ready? When you reach the other side of the bridge, your folks should be waiting in the parking lot for you. I'll follow to wait with you just in case, until I'm sure your rides are here. Let's go Harper."

Harper waited as Kane played the bars of the prelude and the soloist finished, sweetly singing the introductory lyrics, "…joy that will last." The choir erupted in song and the recessional began. Kane banged away a few minutes more after the last kid exited the tent and then he scurried to bring up the rear of the line of carolers who clumped up on the other side of the bridge leaving just enough room for Kane to join them.

He saw Maggie standing near her rental car in animated conversation with a group of women. A zing of happy anticipation at the mere sight of her brought a smile.

"Mom's over there," he said to Harper.

Kane followed in Harper's zooming wake. The little girl crashed into Maggie and wrapped her arms around her waist.

"Whoa," she said. "Hi, Kane. How did the rehearsal go?"

"About as expected," he said wryly. "Are you busy this evening?"

"I'm not sure." Maggie opened the back door for Harper who climbed atop the booster seat and belted herself in. "I heard something about kite flying in Kitty Hawk."

"Yes. They fly lighted kites off Jockey Ridge sand dunes. I thought you might like the birds eye view from my rooftop deck. Maybe after a little dinner? I've been known to do a fair job of grilling steaks."

Maggie closed the back door and then opened the driver's door leaving it ajar. "Harper, too?"

"Sure, if we can't find someone to stay with her. She's always welcome. But I hope we can be alone."

A pretty blush stained her cheeks and a soft smile bloomed on her lips. He loved that the prospect of alone time with him had that effect on her.

"I hope so, too. I'll see what I can do."

"Come over at five? I know it's a bit early for dinner, but they start flying the kites around sunset."

"See you later," she said.

****

Christmas Wish in a Bottle

Kane wasn't much of a chef, but he thought the twice baked potatoes warming in the kitchen oven and the perfectly steamed fresh asparagus he had prepared might impress his lady. He had set a table for two and Christmas instrumentals—piano, of course—played on his rooftop deck. Constellations, a waning crescent moon, and assorted planets shone brightly in the clear velvet-black sky overhead.

The barbecue grill was preheated and ready for the two seasoned filet mignons on a platter in the outdoor refrigerator. A bottle of cabernet sauvignon breathed on the table.

Maggie arrived at five o'clock on the dot without Harper in tow. A group at the inn had folded her under their wings to go to the Kites With Lights event. He suggested that she keep her jacket on until she tested the temperature out on the deck with the pillar gas heater going. She shed her coat immediately after she stepped outside revealing a snug long-sleeved, red tee shirt tucked into jeans which fit her slim, perfect figure enticingly. Everything about the woman magnetized him.

He took her jacket and draped it over his arm, pulled out her chair for her, seated her at the table, hung her coat on her chairback and then set to work grilling the steaks. She reached for the bottle of wine, and he strode over pre-empting pouring a glass for each of them.

"What should we toast to?" she said.

Flickering candlelight played across her delicate features—beautiful.

"To us," he said clinking his goblet against hers.

She followed suit her sparkling green eyes locked on his. "To us," she whispered.

They each took a sip of wine and then Kane returned to the grill holding his glass in hand. Turning the steaks, he looked toward the Sound scanning the skies. "Things are getting pretty interesting now."

"Yeah? What do you see?"

Kane walked toward the deck rail. "Come on over here."

Maggie joined him. He wrapped his arm around her, and she tilted her head leaning against her shoulder. "Oh wow!"

"Yeah, wow." He gazed down at her.

Focusing up at him, she said, "You're not looking at the kites."

"Prettier view right here," he said.

The grill smoked and a charred smell drifted on the air prompting Kane to stride over and remove the steaks. He grinned at her. "Just in time. I'll plate these and run downstairs for the side dishes. I'll be right back."

He finished serving dinner and then sat down opposite Maggie raising his wine glass.

"One more toast. To a goodnight kiss this evening."

She smiled, picked up her glass and tapped it against his. "Ditto."

Chapter 13

Maggie scooped up her notebook from the desk and checked her reflection in the oval mirror over the dresser. The neat French twist styled hairdo and the black turtleneck sweater that she wore projected the business-like image she was going for. Black tailored pants and ballet slippers completed the look.

Harper sat on the bed with Maggie's iPad on her lap watching her favorite Christmas movie, *White Christmas*. A pang of missing her mom hit Maggie. Watching the movie together with her beloved Nana every year was a lifelong tradition for Harper. Mom had held one-year old Harper on her lap watching the film during her first Christmas season. As Harper got a little older, the pair baked cookies or wrapped presents together while the movie played in the background.

She wanted to informally question more guests that morning, so no time for movie watching.

"We need to go down to the breakfast buffet, Harper," Maggie said.

She glanced up at Maggie. "Can I bring your iPad and keep watching the movie?"

"You know the rule about electronics at the table, but I'll make an exception today," Maggie replied, sensitive to Harper's need to feel close to her grandmother. "You can even bring your sketchbook if you want."

Guests congregated around the long kitchen counter where Kay had set out a sumptuous breakfast buffet. After fixing a plate for Harper, Maggie looked around for a place for the two of them to sit. Mike came to the rescue toting a folding table.

"Good morning, ladies. This is the table I set up for the little ones when they visit. I thought Harper might be more comfortable sitting here."

He unfolded the legs and positioned the card table next to the sliding glass door near the long table where the guests were pulling up chairs.

"This is just perfect," Maggie said, grateful for his thoughtfulness.

Kane strode into the kitchen carrying two small chairs, placed the chairs at the "kids' table" and then walked over to Maggie, gave her a hug, and whispered in her ear, "You look pretty this morning."

"Thank you." She thrilled at the sweet compliment. His dark hair was shower-damp and shampoo fragrant. His musky cologne filled Maggie's senses making her dizzy with his nearness.

Harper took a seat at the small table. "Want to sit with me?" she said to Kane.

"I sure do. That's why I brought two chairs. Let me grab some breakfast first. I'll be right back."

Maggie followed Kane to the buffet. "You don't have to sit at the tiny table."

"I know I don't." He loaded a plate with waffles, eggs, and sausages. "I want to."

He smiled, kissed her cheek, and went back to Harper's table. Maggie suppressed a giggle watching him lower awkwardly onto the small chair folding his six-foot frame into a crouched position. If he raised his heels just an inch, he would have elevated the entire table. Kane took some good-natured ribbing from the guests at the adult table.

What a kind man he is.

She poured a mug of coffee, added a splash of milk, and spooned some scrambled eggs onto a plate before finding a vacant seat next to Nancy Conway.

Nancy's fork froze half-way to her open mouth as Kane graced the table with one of his jaw dropping smiles.

"Heavens," Nancy uttered under her breath. "He is a god."

She belted out a laugh. "If only I was twenty years younger."

Maggie instantly liked her. When Kay began clearing empty plates, Maggie said, "Do any of you have a moment to discuss your past stays here at Christmas time?"

Several people made excuses but Nancy and her husband, Ethan stayed seated at the table as well as two men: Brian introduced himself and his husband, Charles.

"I'm Maggie Larsen. I'm not sure if you're aware that I'm here to write an article for *In The Know*."

"We did hear that, didn't we Charley?" Brian said.

Charley nodded. "We love that magazine. I can't believe you might mention us in your article."

"We'll see where our interviews take us." Maggie opened her Moleskine notebook, pen at the ready. "If I tell your story, I'll use first names only. Please let me know if you're uncomfortable with anything I ask. Agreed?"

"Yes."

"Of course."

"I think it's unanimous," Nancy said.

"Great. Thank you." Maggie turned her attention to the woman seated next to her. "Nancy, I believe you told Kay Layton in a letter that you wrote a wish on a slip of paper which you placed in a sea glass bottle that you corked and threw into the ocean. And that wish came true on Christmas day."

"Yes. I know a lot of people think I'm crazy and don't believe me, but I know what happened and I will stand by it."

"We believe you," the men said in unison.

"I'd love to hear your story if you'd like to share it." Maggie sat back and put the pen down to inspire confidence in her discretion.

"I came to the inn with Ethan four years ago." She patted her husband's arm. "It was a getaway from sadness and frustration. Ethan and I fell in love when we were teenagers. I got pregnant when I was sixteen. Our parents didn't care that we wanted to marry and somehow raise our baby together even though we were kids. They made me give up our baby for adoption. Although I pleaded and begged to allow an open adoption so I could find our son or daughter someday, the adoption was closed, and I wasn't permitted to know any details. The delivery was C-section, and they wouldn't let me see the baby. I didn't even know our child's sex.

"Until four years ago.

"When we arrived here at the inn, there was a beautiful green, glass bottle in our room, and I inquired about it. Kay said that the bottle was a little souvenir and was ours to keep. She also said that for fun we might write down a wish, put it in the bottle and send it out to sea.

"I woke up in the middle of the night and felt compelled to do just that. It was the day before Christmas. I did it! I felt a strange sense of peace flinging that bottle in the ocean."

"And your wish came true? Are you willing to share what you wrote in the note?" Maggie said, her tone soft.

Nancy remained silent for a while. Maggie sat patiently giving her time to elaborate or decline to answer.

"I wished that my child would come to me."

Maggie resisted rolling her eyes or arching her eyebrows anticipating what would come next. "And did you find your child here at the inn?"

Nancy shot Ethan a knowing smile. "After the beautiful brunch Kay prepared for us on Christmas morning, we went for a walk on the beach where we discovered a bottle just like mine washed up on shore. Except there was no paper inside and there was a cork in the bottle, so it couldn't have been mine. I picked it up and decided to bring it home with me since making my wish had already made me feel more peaceful and accepting."

Tears welled in Nancy's eyes. "When we returned to our room, I checked my emails. We had registered with an online adoption reunion registry and had provided all the details I had about the baby's birth as one of the many avenues we took to try to locate our child. On Christmas Day four years ago, I received an email notifying us that our twenty-one-year-old son was trying to find us!"

Nancy heaved a breath. "So, despite what anyone might say, I know in my heart that my wish came true.

Our son is a wonderful young man."

Incredulity warred with wonder in Maggie. She reached out and clasped Nancy's hand, tears brimming. Brian swiped away tears with his palms. No one uttered a sound as Ethan wrapped an arm around his wife's shoulder smiling broadly.

"I could use a cup of tea. Anyone else want anything?" Maggie broke the silence.

She needed a moment to collect her thoughts. When she had first read the letters attributing magical happenings to floating wishes in bottles, she had no idea what shape her article would take since she hadn't believed the claims for a moment.

Now I don't know what to think. How could any of this be plausible?

Maggie drifted over to the counter, poured hot water from the electric kettle over a peppermint tea bag, and returned to the table.

"Well," Brian said. "I guess it's our turn."

"It is. I'd love to hear your story," Maggie urged him.

"Charley and I fell in love when we were in college. We married as soon as it was legal in Minnesota. We had a wonderful life but we both thought something was missing. We wanted children.

"Charley is a highly successful lawyer." Brian gazed at his spouse starry-eyed. "He started the process for us to adopt. It was hard with so many disappointments. Then a miracle happened. A teenage unwed pregnant mother was very near delivering, and she agreed to an adoption. To say we were over the moon is an understatement. We decorated the nursery. I went absolutely crazy buying things."

Charley laughed. "Now that, my love, is an understatement."

"Then we got a call." The color drained out of Brian's face and Charley put his arm around his shoulder pulling him closer to him. "The birth mother had changed her mind because we're gay."

Maggie and Nancy gasped at the same time.

"No way," Nancy said.

"Yes way. We were crushed. The house was ready for our baby's arrival. We couldn't stand looking at the nursery. We had to get away. A friend recommended the Inn of the Three Butterflies. Here our stories are similar." Brian took Nancy's hand and gave it a squeeze. "I too woke in the middle of the night to write down a wish and toss the bottle into the ocean. I simply wished for a child of our own. I didn't find the bottle. Charley did on his morning beach jog. It was empty but still corked.

"He brought the bottle back to our room. We were seated at Christmas dinner when Charley's phone rang. It was the birth mother. She said she was wrong. She dreamed that her baby belonged with us. And the best part was that she was in the hospital getting ready to give birth. We made a few calls, booked a private plane out of Manteo and we flew to Minnesota in time to be at the hospital when our little boy was born."

Although Brian beamed as he related his story, tears streaked his face.

"I'm afraid to ask," Maggie said quietly. "Where is your little one now?"

"We rent a house here on the beach for Christmas every year since Sebastian was born. He'll be three years old on Christmas Day. Our parents are staying with us at the house and so is Sebastian's birth mother. We have included her in our family. You can never have too many people to love a child."

Maggie glanced at the card table. Kane wrapped his arm around Harper and pointed to something she was drawing. Truer words were never spoken.

"I can't thank you enough for sharing your stories." Maggie pushed back from the table and the couples followed suit.

On impulse, Maggie gave Nancy, Ethan, Brian, and Charles warm hugs. After they left, she drifted over to the window and stared out at the waves lost in thought.

****

Kane focused on Maggie's silhouette as she stood stock still, leaning a shoulder against the window jamb. He extricated himself from the cramped position on the miniature chair with a slight groan and ambled over to her.

He gently placed his hands on her shoulders, spinning her to face him. "Everything all right, pretty lady?"

His heart shredded at the sight of her tear-tracked face. "Aw, please don't cry," he said cupping her cheeks with his hands and wiping the tears away with his thumbs. "Whatever's hurting you, I'll fix it."

She gave him a wan smile that didn't reach her emerald-colored eyes. "I'm just not sure if this is right."

Kane's stomach sank. How had he made her question their relationship? "What did I do, Maggie?"

"You?" She knit her brow.

"Come sit down."

Kane pulled out a chair at the "adult" table and then took a seat across from her. "Now, what's not right?"

Maggie wagged her head frowning.

"Sweetheart. Let me help you if I can."

"I don't think I want to do this story anymore."

"What has upset you so much about writing the article?" He extended his hands across the table, gratified that she accepted the handhold.

"When I learned about the wishes in bottles, I honestly thought the claims were nuts. Did people really believe that their lives changed because of a piece of paper in a bottle? But I always do my research work with an open mind."

"I have no doubt. And now?"

"Now after meeting the guests and hearing their stories, I believe them. I don't want to expose them to scrutiny, or worse, ridicule. I can understand why Carol hesitated to talk to me and why she was a surprised that your aunt gave me the letters in the first place." She heaved a sigh. "I'm sorry, Kane. I'm not being logical. I have a job to do, and I will just have to do it."

He raised her hand to his lips and kissed it getting a whiff of her floral perfume stirring longing deep in his soul. Kane wanted to sweep her into his arms and bury his face in her neck.

"You don't have to do anything you don't feel comfortable doing." He paused, mulling her situation over. "What if you avoided writing about the personal stories completely? You were moved by the candy bomber, weren't you? Do you think your readers would be touched by that story? I'm sure Karin would agree to an interview. It would be a win, win," he said warming up to the idea. "You would still have a heartfelt Christmas story and maybe the publicity would increase fundraising for her to keep the bomber flying."

Maggie pursed her lips, her eyes downcast. A smile

slowly appeared on her face. "That might actually be a brilliant idea. My boss never mentioned the wishes when assigning the article in the first place. I can slant the entire piece around all the charitable events here during the holiday season."

She jumped up and skirted the table. "I could kiss you," she said leaning down toward him.

Kane figured that she intended to buss his cheek, but he preempted her, moving his head so that her lips landed squarely on his. He forgot that guests or his family could happen upon their lip lock at any moment or that her little girl who sat a few feet away coloring at the table could turn around and catch him kissing her mom.

And the intensity of Maggie's kiss proved that she was as carried away as he was.

But propriety won out and he reluctantly ended the kiss and whispered in her ear, "I wish we were alone."

She wore a dreamy expression on her beautiful face. "Me too."

Chapter 14

"Here," Skye said piling dresses on hangers into Maggie's arms. "Try these on for now and I'll keep searching."

Maggie looked askance at Skye while she juggled the heavy bundle of clothes. "You don't think I'll find one that I like out of all of these?"

Skye didn't give Maggie as much as a glance. Instead, she strode from rack to rack in the brand name outlet store riffling through the size six and small dresses in the shop. "Ooh, I like this one. Here."

"Whoa." Maggie balanced the load and staggered into the dressing room.

She hooked the dress hangers onto a bar on the wall, unzipped her jacket and hung it on a hook on the back of the dressing room door. A tap sounded and Maggie opened the door met with Skye shoving another dress toward Maggie. "This is the one! Try it on first, OK? I'll wait out here."

"You don't think it's too revealing…and clingy?" Maggie eyed the green satin cocktail dress.

"No, I think it's perfect for the Christmas Eve Concert. It's at the mansion, after all, and you can't find a more formal venue on the whole sandbar. There's a champagne reception in the ballroom afterwards for the adults," came Skye's muted voice from behind the door.

"Oh wow, I didn't know about that." Maggie kicked

off her flats, shimmying out of her jeans and pulling her sweater off over her head. "What about all the kids in the choir…and Harper?"

She unzipped the dress, slipped it off the hanger, and tried it on.

"They have their own party in the solarium. Hot chocolate, Christmas cookies and candy canes. They also play games for prizes."

"Harper will love that. What a wonderful tradition." Maggie swung open the dressing room door. "What do you think?"

She beamed at Maggie clapping her hands together. "First try. It's perfect. Do you like it?"

Maggie turned around to check out the fit in the mirror leaving the door ajar. "I kind of love it." She about-faced and gazed at the reflection of the back of the dress over her right shoulder.

The silky, emerald-colored material skimmed her body draping softly over her hips to mid-calf. She struck several poses assessing the fit from all angles.

"Kane will grovel at your feet when he sees you in that dress," Skye asserted.

A hot blush crept up Maggie's neck and face. "He's not…I mean we're not…"

Skye held out her arm showing Maggie the palm of her hand—stop. "Not blind, Maggie," she quipped. "I know my cousin. He's crazy about you."

She didn't know what to say to that. But she loved the thought. She bent her elbows up over her head and reached behind her to unzip the dress.

"Here, let me help you with that," Skye said.

Maggie dropped her arms and turned around obediently. The cool rush of air on her back as the zipper lowered sent a chill through her. Or was it a thrill that zipped through her at the prospect of crazy-in-love Kane groveling at her feet? She couldn't remember the last time she felt so much happy anticipation of basking in a man's attention in a sexy dress with Christmas lights aglow. Maggie hoped Skye was right about Kane's feelings for her. Because she was crazy about him, too, and had begun to dream about more with him. A man to love her and her girl with whom Maggie could build a life, a family, children of their own.

It was a beautiful dream.

Carefully draping the party dress back on the hanger, she changed back into her clothes her heart winging, contemplating wowing Kane on the night of the concert. She stepped out of the dressing room carrying her prize to the register to check out.

"Do you need to look for anything? I'd love to help. Actually, with your coloring this dress would probably suit you better than me," she said to Skye. "And we're both probably the same size."

"Nope. That dress was made for you. I have a sapphire-colored velvet dress to wear that night that Gabe loves. Snapped it up on sale early in the year."

Maggie gladly presented her credit card to the cashier, even though she rarely bought anything for herself. Pleased that she found the perfect dress at outlet store prices, Maggie followed Skye out the door with her plastic encased prize hung over her arm. "Can I stow this in your car before we do some more shopping?"

"Of course."

A couple of bleeps sounded and the locks on Skye's minivan disengaged with a loud click. Maggie spread her dress bag out on the back seat and then relocked the car.

She turned toward Skye. "Where next?"

"The kids' store here is adorable. They sell clothes and toys and shoes. I want to do some more shopping for my girls."

"Sounds good. Also, do you think you might help me choose a gift for your parents? They've been so kind to me and Harper."

"Of course. Mom's favorite store is down the way. There's also a music store along this strip. I don't know if they'd have anything to interest Harper, but maybe."

"That's great. I hope they sell PadMus there."

"What's that?" Skye said, holding open the door to the children's store for Maggie.

"It's an electronic tablet for reading and writing sheet music. I thought it might be too advanced for her this year, but seeing her at the piano with Kane, I think she'd love working with it and is ready to use it."

Skye chuckled following Maggie into the shop. "He'll probably steal it from her."

After several trips loading packages in Skye's car, the women declared that they were shopped out. Maggie checked her cell phone. "It's one o'clock already!"

"Time flies when you're having fun," they chorused.

"Nothing more fun than spending money," Skye said.

"Do you have time for me to treat you to lunch?" Maggie said. "Or do you need to get back to the triplets?"

"Mom said to spend the whole day away if we needed it, so I'm good. What about Harper?"

"Kane volunteered to spend the day with Harper starting with her practice session at his house, a concert rehearsal, apparently peanut butter and jelly sandwiches for lunch and beach time depending on what time I return."

"Cool. I love a vegan restaurant here. Want to go there?"

"Perfect. My treat," Maggie said climbing into the passenger seat of Skye's van.

Skye triggered the ignition. "No way. We'll split the bill."

"Please, I'd like to buy you lunch. You've taken care of Harper so many times. It's the least I can do."

"Oh, that's nothing. She's a darling and I really appreciate her help with the girls. They adore her."

"It's mutual, but I insist."

"OK. But next time, my treat."

"Deal."

Settled at a table on a charming, fairy-lights decorated deck overlooking the Sound, Maggie perused the menu.

"If you're in the mood for a little pig-out, the thin crust pizza here is fantastic," Skye said.

Maggie tossed her menu on the table. "Pig-out it is. You choose the toppings. I like everything except green peppers and mushrooms."

"Are you sure we're not related? I can't stand those, either." Skye placed the order for the pie, and then asked the waiter to wait a minute.

"Are you in the mood for an afternoon splurge, Maggie?" she said.

"What do you have in mind?"

"A glass of wine? I hardly ever get to act like an adult anymore chasing after my girls."

"I'd love a glass of wine."

"Chardonnay OK?"

"You read my mind."

"Two glasses of chardonnay, also, please," she said to the waiter.

The wine was fruity and buttery adding a festive touch to the rare girls' day out. The pizza was delicious—almost as good as Chicago pizza.

"So," Maggie said setting down her wine glass. "I haven't met your husband yet. Is he at work?"

"Yes. He was in Washington until the 15th and then made a stop at his horse farm. He'll be home tomorrow. I can't wait."

"He's a rancher, then?"

"Oh, not at all. He's a senator. His family owns a horse farm in Virginia. My mother-in-law is a widow and Gabe checks in at the farm whenever he can."

"Wait. Virginia? Are you married to Gabriel Hartley?"

Skye's eyes danced and a huge smile bloomed on her face. "Uh huh."

"Wow, Skye. He's so…"

"Gorgeous? Handsome? A real hunk?"

Maggie nodded, grinning at Skye. "I was about to say, he's so dedicated to his job."

She burst out laughing. "No, you weren't, but he is that, too. But…speaking of gorgeous, handsome hunks, your man is no slouch."

My man. "I think maybe it's a little soon to think of Kane as…mine."

"Not really. I believe in love at first sight since I met Gabe."

"Aw, so romantic. How did you meet?"

Her face brightened with her grin. "I was standing in a ballroom at a rehearsal dinner for my best friend's wedding and he came up to me, took me into his arms and kissed me stupid."

"Wait, what? You had never met before and...he just, what, swept you off your feet?"

Skye picked an olive off her slice of pizza and popped it in her mouth. "Nope, never met him before. And he sure as hell swept me off my feet. Long story, but it was a heck of a kiss.

"Anyway, back to Kane. I disagree that it's too soon for him to have fallen for you, Maggie. I see the way he looks at you. And how downright sociable he is since you've been around."

"He's usually anti-social?"

"Not exactly. More the reclusive, dark prodigy, leave me to my music type. Anyway, I don't think I've ever seen him so...happy. Yeah, that's the difference."

She couldn't help grinning at the thought that she made Kane happy.

"I don't want to pry," Skye said.

"Yes, you do," Maggie interjected on a laugh.

"Well, OK, I do. Is it painful to talk about your husband? Did you divorce? Please tell me he didn't die."

"No, I've never been married."

She was reluctant to continue having never talked about Harper's conception and the tragic deaths of the couple that would have been Harper's parents in every way except biological. But Maggie was falling for Kane and if Skye was right about how Kane felt about her, Skye might someday become family to her and Harper.

Maggie took a deep breath and dove into telling her story. "I conceived Harper through in vitro fertilization. I was a surrogate for my sister Eileen and her husband Greg. Eileen had survived ovarian cancer and Greg had beaten prostate cancer. They asked me for my help because they wanted desperately to have a family. They were so excited when I became pregnant."

Skye furrowed her brow. "Were?"

Although five years had passed since the plane crash, the memory of loss would always remain fresh for her, and tears stung the corners of Maggie's eyes.

"Oh, don't, sweetie." Skye reached over the table and clasped Maggie's hand. "If it's too hard for you to talk about, don't say another word. I don't want to make you cry."

She blotted her eyes with a napkin. "Thank you. But I'm fine, really. Eileen was my only sibling and I just adored her. Eileen and Greg asked me to be an egg donor. I didn't hesitate to agree for a second. They had planned to search for a surrogate mother, but I volunteered immediately to carry their child."

"Was your brother-in-law the biological father?"

"No. Greg was sterile, also, from his cancer treatment. His roommate in college had already agreed to donate sperm prior to their asking me. I was eight and half months pregnant when they died in a plane crash island hopping in Hawaii."

"Oh, Maggie, that is awful. I'm so, so sorry."

"Thank you, Skye. It was a terrible time. They were ecstatic anticipating becoming parents and went on a "babymoon" to see the Hawaiian islands. When I received the phone call notifying me that they had died, I blacked out and I guess I started hemorrhaging. I was rushed to the hospital for an emergency c-section. When I woke up, I was a single mother. It wasn't what I wanted, of course. I always thought of Harper as Eileen's and Greg's child the whole time I carried her. I had planned to be the best aunt ever. Harper is a miracle to me in so many ways. Loving her and raising her has helped me heal. My parents, too."

"I'll bet. Have you ever met Harper's biological father?"

"No. I'm not sure about the details of his sperm donation. All I know is that his name is Joe, and that he and Greg were in school together in New Haven."

"New Haven, Connecticut? Yale?"

"Uh huh. The School of Music—kind of a big deal when Greg was accepted. Greg was a music professor in Chicago."

Skye's mouth fell open and her eyes widened.

Maggie frowned at her strange reaction. "Are you all right?"

"Um…yes. I'm good." She dropped her eyes seemingly gazing intently on the half-eaten pizza. "Thank you for sharing, Maggie. It's a very sad but wonderful story. Harper is a darling."

"She is my heart," Maggie said.

Chapter 15

Kane's mood brightened when he spied Harper perched on the inn's porch next to his uncle. Her sunny disposition consistently made him smile. He parked, cut the engine, and sprung out of the truck eager to spend the day with his little protégé.

"Good morning, Uncle Mike. Hey there, Harper," Kane said.

Harper gave Mike a hug and then bounded down the stairs to meet Kane.

He took her hand and helped her step up into the backseat. "First, we'll rehearse for the concert and then I thought we could grab lunch. How does that sound?"

"Good," she said climbing into the booster seat.

Kane latched her seatbelt and then shut the door carefully thinking about his dad's routine before road trips when he was a kid. After fastening his little sister's seatbelt, Dad always turned to Mom and said, "Precious cargo secure."

Kane understood that Maggie had entrusted him with precious cargo and drove under the speed limit as he merged onto the beach road. He glimpsed Harper's reflection in the rearview mirror. She had earphones on, her eyes were closed, and she smiled softly as she undoubtedly listened to music—his kindred spirit.

Her smile, so like her mother's, touched his heart. Thoughts of Maggie dominated his waking moments.

Dreams at night were filled with her laughter and smile. His mind wandered to reliving their time together and anticipating more to come even when he was at the piano. The reverie wasn't exclusive to Maggie. Harper had captured his heart, too.

Who knew that he'd experience sweet happiness anticipating spending the day with a kindergartner?

Traffic thinned as the truck neared the four-wheel-drive beach fronting the property where the concert would take place. Locals were unhappy when a developer secured the permits to build the massive house with twenty-four, bedroom suites dubbing it The Mansion. After its completion, rather than the anticipated eyesore, The Mansion became a sought-after venue for weddings and events. The owner had respected the natural beauty of the dunes and constructed an overflow parking area in the neighboring town. Electric shuttles transported guests from the remote lot.

After years of visiting OBX, Kane knew every shortcut. He drove up the rocky driveway used for deliveries in the back of the building. He helped Harper out of the truck quickly, having glimpsed "visitors" on the beach. Raising his index finger to his lips, he shushed her, took her hand, and led her to a beach vantage point. Three horses moved slowly along the water's edge.

Harper's eyes widened in surprise as she watch the majestic animals pass by.

She didn't speak until they had entered the mansion. "The horses are beautiful," she exclaimed rushing to a window for another look. "Why are they loose on the beach? Where are their owners?"

"They're wild horses, Harper, nobody owns them. People say they descended from the Spanish mustangs brought by explorers over five hundred years ago."

"Wow. Do you think they'll come back?" she said turning away from the window.

"Maybe. If they do, I'll try to take a few photos for you."

A petite woman with pixie-cut, red hair rushed towards Kane, her high heels clicking on the tile floor. "Kane, I'm so glad to see you. I can't thank you enough for all you've done. It leaves me speechless."

She threw her arms around him and squeezed. "You have no idea how many lives you will change this Christmas. The children who will find presents under their trees…"

She took a step back freeing him from her perfume laden hug, beaming at him. "Thank you so much for paying for everything so we can use all the proceeds from ticket sales for the community. You're my hero this holiday."

Her effusive praise made his cheeks burn with embarrassment.

"Just helping my neighbors," he muttered. "Thank *you* for moving swiftly to rearrange things. The predicted winds on concert day would probably blow the tent down. I think *you're* the hero," he said turning the tables on her.

Mavis dipped her gaze shyly. "Oh, thanks. You're too kind. Come with me. I can't wait for you to see the ballroom," she said grabbing hold of his hand.

Kane linked hands with Harper as Mavis led them towards a pair of carved mahogany doors. Mavis let loose his handhold and shoved open the doors revealing the ornate ballroom in the process of transformation.

"Oh, it's so pretty!" Harper said.

"It is, isn't it?" Mavis agreed.

Dimly lit crystal chandeliers and wall sconces bathed the space with a warm glow. Rows of padded chairs situated off both sides of a wide center aisle. Risers were mounted on a newly constructed stage. Workmen twined twinkling lights on Christmas trees on either end of the stage and hung lit green wreaths with giant red bows on the stage backdrop and along the walls of the audience area.

"We just opened the boxes with the choir robes that you ordered. They're perfect. Did Kathy tell you that we sold out? Did you know that she contacted the college and their IT club volunteered to manage live streaming the concert? Or that Holy Redeemer by the Sea is going to show the concert for free, but they will pass baskets in case people want to donate?"

Kane might have responded but Mavis didn't take a breath in her obvious excitement.

"We have *never* had such a response before. I guess it helps to have a Grammy winner perform," she rambled.

Kane almost heaved a relieved sigh when the kids and adults clamored into the room and rushed the stage to climb onto the risers. *So much for an orderly candlelight procession.*

"Time to get to work," he said.

Mavis made a few shoo motions with her hands. "Of course. I won't keep you."

Kane and Harper walked down the aisle towards the two pianos center stage in front of the risers. He owed Skye and Gabe a big thank you for getting the pianos here in time for the rehearsal.

Harper sat at her piano observing Kane accompany

the choirs' rehearsal. During the performance, Harper wouldn't join Kane onstage until they played their duet, *Magic Christmas Bells* in the finale.

He dismissed the singers after a couple hours' work, happy with their progress and then practiced the duet with Harper, who had the music down perfectly.

"Would you like to stay on stage after our performance and play with me for a sing-along? I have sheet music for you if you're interested."

"Yes." She gave him the sweetest smile reminding him of Maggie. He realized that next to composing, making Maggie and Harper smile was what he wanted most to do.

"We can go back to my house after lunch and practice for a while."

"What would you like for lunch?" Kane said as he steered the truck onto the beach road.

"French fries."

"And what would you like with your French fries?"

"Ketchup."

Kane hooted a laugh. "I think you need a little more than French fries and ketchup. How about we add a hamburger to that?"

"How about a grilled cheese sandwich?"

"Deal. I know just the place."

He pulled over to the side of the road, parked and placed an online order with the local Hamburger Heaven.

Ten minutes later he picked up his order at the drive-through. On the way home, the smell of fries had his stomach growling.

In the kitchen, he handed Harper paper plates and napkins to carry out to the table on the deck. He even sliced an apple to give her what he hoped was a mom-approved healthy addition to the meal. They gobbled down the food in minutes.

"Can I ask you something?" Harper said after wiping her mouth quite ladylike with a napkin.

"Of course. You can ask me anything."

"Do you think the Christmas wishes in the bottles are real?"

"Hmm," he hedged. What would Maggie say? Should he dodge the question and advise Harper to ask her mom instead? Was the very real magic of the Inn of the Three Butterflies believable for a kid and her logical mother?

His parents had frankly answered his innocent questions as a child and had taught him that honesty was paramount. How could he not believe in magic? Magic had encompassed his entire life.

"Yes," he said. "I do believe that the guests your mom has interviewed had their wishes come true. I don't know how, but I believe in magic."

"Good," she said, her features serious.

She hoisted her backpack up from under the table, opened the zipper and extracted her notebook and a colored pencil. "Will you help me send a wish in a bottle, please?"

It seemed an innocent enough request. But would Maggie approve his advising her daughter to make some far-flung wish and risk crushing disappointment?

"Maybe we should run this by your mom first?"

Harper's shoulders drooped and she looked like she was on the verge of tears. "I want it to be a surprise for Mommy," she lamented.

How could he say no to that face?

"Surprise it is. What do you want me to do to help?"

"I'll write my wish down first." She gripped her pencil tightly and bent over her notebook.

Kane cleared the table, brought the trash into the kitchen, and then sat down next to Harper. He side-eyed her paper and made out the letter D.

Harper noticed Kane's focus and shielded the paper with her tiny hand. "No peeking or my wish won't come true."

"Sorry. I won't look again." He took his phone out of his pocket and googled breeders, positive that Harper was in the process of wishing for a dog.

"How do you spell only?" she said, laying her pencil down.

"O.N.L.Y."

"Darn it. I spelled it wrong." She crumpled up her paper and bent over a blank sheet.

Should he search for a puppy or a shelter dog? Maggie might need some convincing, but he was sure he could make her come around to make the sweet kid's wish come true. He'd call the shelter in the morning and see if they had any puppies—after he had Maggie's agreement.

A waft of wind blew Harper's balled-up paper off the table. Kane scooped up the paper rolling at his feet and stuffed it in his pocket.

"All done," she said, carefully rolling her paper into a tube.

"Let's go inside. I think I have just what you need to officially make your wish."

He owed Skye an apology for the complaints about dust collectors he had voiced after she had arranged a dozen vintage bottles on a bookshelf in his study.

Harper inspected each one in the collection and then

chose a long-necked bottle with an etching of a pelican.

"This one is so pretty. Can I use it? When it comes back empty you can have it back."

"That's the one I would have chosen."

Kane's phone vibrated in his pocket. He glanced at the text message. "Great timing. Your mom is back at the inn. Let's get your stuff together and we can walk there on the beach. That way you can find the perfect spot to throw your bottle."

He uncorked the bottle and Harper carefully inserted her paper tube inside. Kane replaced the cork and handed over the bottle.

She held her treasure in both hands tramping through the sand beside him with her head turned toward the sea scanning the waves. Halfway back to the inn, she halted, faced the water, and closed her eyes.

"This is where I think I should send my wish. This feels right," she said holding out the bottle in his direction. "Would you throw it for me? You can throw it much further than I can."

"I would be honored." Kane placed her backpack and shoes on the sand and waded into the waves, ignoring the water soaking through his sneakers and the bottom of his pants. He heaved the bottle into the ocean one-handed as hard as he could, and then sloshed back to Harper.

She jumped up and down grinning widely. "That was the *best* throw. Thank you."

"You are very welcome."

Kane picked up her things and they resumed walking. When they got closer to the inn, he spied Maggie standing and waving on the deck. Harper took off running. Kane jogged behind her and followed

Harper up the stairs.

She launched herself into her mother's arms.

"Did you have a good day?" Maggie said.

"I did. I had fries for lunch."

"And grilled cheese and I even cut up an apple," Kane added. "How about you, Maggie? Did you enjoy your day?"

"I did. I had wine for lunch. Thank you for watching Harper for me so I could go shopping. I really enjoyed spending time with Skye."

"I'm glad. Harper and I got a lot done today." He winked at Harper. "I better head back. I have some business calls to make and work to do. I'll catch up with you tomorrow."

Maggie gave him a soft kiss on the cheek which made him regret that he had to leave.

Kane jogged home in his saturated, squishing sneakers. He kicked them off at the door, dried his feet on a kitchen towel and then padded to his bedroom to ditch the wet pants. Emptying his pockets on his dresser, he flattened out Harper's discarded paper on the top of his chest of drawers.

She had spelled only, onely—an understandable mistake for her age, he figured.

Blood drained from his face as he read her entire wish. He slumped down on the bed, the paper dangling in his hand. *Oh no, what did I do?*

Chapter 16

The doorbell chimed a moment after Kane had taken a seat at the piano to finish his work so that he could search out Maggie and spend a sweet afternoon with her doing whatever her heart desired. Prickling at the interruption, he skipped using the intercom and flew down two flights of stairs to deal quickly with the unexpected visitor. Since it was just shy of lunchtime, he expected to greet a sandwich-platter or casserole-bearing, flirty neighbor lady when he opened the door.

Instead, Skye, balancing a triplet on her hip and Gabe, toting a daughter in each arm, stood on his front porch. A gigantic candy cane striped Santa-bag sat on the ground between them. The kids were dressed identically in tiny jeans and long-sleeved Christmas red shirts. Coupled with their flame-red hair, they looked every bit the miniature firebrands that they were, and their red-headed mom, the grown-up version. Trouble on his doorstep, he thought, amused.

Gabe and Kane met eye-to-eye looking more like brothers than cousins by marriage.

"Hi." Kane ran a hand through his hair mulling over his probable absent-mindedness. "Did I forget that we made plans to get together when you're in town, Gabe?"

Gabe gave him a thin smile. "I take it Skye didn't call, or should I say warn you first?"

Kane knit his brow. "Um. No… Anyway, come in."

He stepped aside and the little family moved past him into his foyer. Skye set down her squirmy bundle on the floor remaining tethered to the toddler with a firm handhold. She regarded her husband. "Darling, will you take the girls out back for a bit while Kane and I talk?"

"Sure," Gabe said. "Come here, Serenity and walk with Daddy."

The little imp obeyed sweet as syrup, trotting next to her dad toward the back of the house.

"What's with the big bag out there?" Kane said.

"Oh." Skye turned around and looked out the door that he had left ajar. "Can you bring that in for me? I want to put presents under your tree."

"What tree?" He lugged in the bag, set it on the floor inside and swung closed the door.

"I'll take care of that, too, before Christmas."

"But we don't exchange gifts. Do you want to start doing that this year?"

"They're not for you." Skye held an index finger up in the air watching Gabe and the kids scramble out onto the deck. "Little ears. They may not talk much yet, but I'm convinced that they're eaves-dropping sponges.

"OK, good, they're out of earshot," she said. "I'm sorry to barge in on you like this, but I really need to talk with you. You know me. I can't wait if it's something important."

"Sure. No problem." He stood rooted to the spot utterly confused about his involvement in what could possibly be too important to wait. "Uh. Do you want to talk here, or go sit down? Would you like something to drink or eat?"

She touched his arm lightly. "No, no. Don't go to any trouble. Let's go sit in your den. I can keep an eye on Gabe and the kids from there. Is that all right?"

"Of course."

He paced by her side making small talk. "Is Gabe here for the holidays?"

"He is. He just arrived a few minutes ago."

Kane furrowed his brow trying to absorb the implication of Skye's dragging her family to his house minutes after being reunited. Despite her odd behavior, he was glad she was there. He wanted to get her take on his aiding and abetting Harper's impossible wish before he told Maggie about it.

Skye took a seat in an armchair and he sat down on an identical chair on the opposite end of a coffee table from her position.

"So…" Skye's gaze was penetrating like twin, jade-colored laser beams. "You went to college in New Haven, right? And you were really close with your roommate?"

The innocuous questions threw Kane off. *What the heck has her looking so serious?*

"Yeah. I met him freshman year and we bonded from the first day. We both majored in music at Yale undergrad and were accepted in the graduate program at Yale School of Music. Why?"

"Just bear with me here." She stared at her lap.

That was not the take-no-prisoners Skye Layton Hartley sitting before him. "Skye…"

The sliding door swished open, and Gabe ambled inside linked to a handhold chain of the triplets. "Sorry to interrupt. Skye. Serenity just swallowed a live, or possibly freshly squished, ant. Do I worry?"

"I like it. I eat it," Serenity declared.

Skye covered her mouth and snorted into her hand.

The men burst out laughing.

"Uh, I think we're fine." Her voice shook with mirth. "Protein."

"Gotcha. I thought so. Just wanted to be sure." Gabe reversed retracing his steps with his tribe and shoved the slider closed behind them.

"Wow," Skye swiped laugh-tears away from her eyes. "That one will be the death of me."

Kane arched an eyebrow. "I'm pretty sure I know who she takes after."

She gave him a crooked grin. "Yep. I apologize to Mom on average four times a day. Where were we?"

"Talking about my roommate, Greg, for some reason."

"Right. Greg. Your roommate's name *was* Greg. Didn't Greg get sick while you were in school?"

"Yeah. Extremely aggressive prostate cancer. It came out of nowhere. It didn't run in his family or anything. He went through hell treating it, but he survived. Amazing. It truly was a miracle. I lost touch with him when I lived in California. And then I learned through our alumni group that he had died in a plane crash. So sad when he had beaten unbelievable odds to live after cancer. What's this all about, Skye?"

"Just a couple more questions. I promise I'll explain."

"All right, shoot."

"Maybe we weren't supposed to know this, but Aunt Kamille told Mom when you donated sperm for Greg because he hoped to become a father someday. They both thought it was wonderful of you."

"Yeah, well. It wasn't a secret and no big deal to help him out, but yes. I did."

"One more question. Were you still calling yourself, Joe when you were in college?"

Kane huffed a laugh. "I was."

She nodded. "I remember how much you hated your proper name and as a little boy you said you wanted to be called "Joe", short for your middle name, Joseph, not a "Hurrikane". You insisted. Nobody in the family did at first."

"And I pitched fits and refused to answer to anything but Joe. Mom finally relented when I came home with a black eye from fighting a bully who taunted me about my name. She told the grammar schoolteacher to go along with me, so it became official. Even my high school diploma reads Joseph Binder Martin."

She pursed her lips. "I knew I was right. Listen, Kane, Maggie—"

"Oh, wait a minute," he interjected. Hearing Maggie's name reminded him about Harper's Christmas wish. "Before you continue, can I show you something and ask your advice—as a parent of little girls?"

"Uh," Skye seemed to flounder for a moment. "Sure."

"Be right back."

Kane hurried upstairs to his bedroom where he retrieved Harper's original written wish.

He hurried back down to the den and handed the paper to Skye. "Harper wrote this yesterday and discarded it because of a misspelling. She wanted to make a Christmas wish in a bottle. I not only helped her by letting her use one of those vintage bottles you chose to decorate my study, but also, I pitched the bottle into the ocean for her when she found the ideal spot. I'm afraid Maggie will kill me when she learns that I encouraged Harper with this far-fetched wish."

Skye finished scanning the note and rounded her eyes. "Wow. I'm amazed."

Kane narrowed his eyes. "I'm in big trouble with Maggie, right?"

"No…uh…" she stammered wagging her head. "How in the heck does my mom *do* this?"

"Your mom? What does Aunt Kay have to do with this?"

"I have been trying to piece this together for years and I've only gotten as far as noticing that only a newcomer each year has had a wish fulfilled. Does Mom bring certain people here? This year the only newcomers are Maggie and Harper. Huh…" she rambled staring blankly out at the ocean.

"Skye?" He waved a hand in front of her face gaining her attention.

She focused on him, bestowing him with a dazzling smile. "Little cousin, you're going to give Harper the *best* Christmas of her life. By the way, the bag of presents that you carried inside are for Harper from you. I went shopping on your behalf as soon as I figured everything out."

Kane sat back heavily in his seat. "You bought gifts for me to give to Harper? Uh…thanks. But what the heck, Skye?"

"This is going to come as a shock, Kane, but hear me out." She scooched up to the edge of her seat. "Gabe is here for a father-to-father conversation if you need it."

He blinked struggling to grasp the point of Skye's strange rambling. *Father-to-father?*

"As you know Maggie and I spent yesterday together. Over lunch I asked Maggie about her past and she told me about Harper's father."

That revelation more than spurred his interest. "Really? Go on."

"Maggie's sister Eileen survived ovarian cancer and wasn't able to conceive or carry a child of her own. She met her husband, a fellow cancer survivor, at a fundraising event. Maggie agreed not only to donate eggs so that her sister and brother-in-law could become parents, but also volunteered to be their surrogate to carry the baby. Eileen's husband's name was Greg and his roommate Joe donated sperm so that Greg might become a father."

Kane's jaw dropped as the information sank in. "Harper is…"

Skye zipped over to him, crouched next to his chair, and grabbed hold of his hand. "Harper is Maggie's and your biological child."

"Harper is mine…" He trailed off, at a loss for words.

"Are you OK? Do you want to talk with Gabe for a bit? How are you feeling? What do you need?"

"I…" He gazed at her blankly. "I'm not sure how I feel."

She knelt and sat back on her heels looking up at him. "Isn't it amazing that Harper is here sending a wish to the universe for a daddy to love her and her mommy? I'm pretty sure you already do…love her and her mommy. You can give Harper her wish."

"Yes…" Kane marveled at the truth of that admission.

Disjointed thoughts swirled through his mind.

Harper is my little girl. No wonder I was drawn to Maggie and Harper from the first minute I saw them.

And Harper's talent at the piano? She's exactly like me at that age. Maggie has green eyes and blonde hair, and Harper looks like me with her black hair and blue eyes. Why didn't I make the connection before this?

Gabe and the kids barged into the room. "You told him, Skye?"

"I did."

"You need my help here, Kane?"

Kane stared at him in a daze. "I think I'm good."

"It's a lot, Kane. But if you want to fulfill the role of Harper's dad, and Maggie lets you, I guarantee it will bring you so much happiness," Gabe assured him.

If Maggie lets me. "Does Maggie know?"

Skye took Gabe's hand. He towed her to her feet. "No. I wasn't a hundred percent sure I had it right until I confirmed my suspicions with you. But it has to be true. All the puzzle pieces fit."

He nodded, beaming at her and Gabe. "Yes. You're right. She's very like me, isn't she?"

"Look at you, proud papa," she teased.

"What do you think I should do? Just tell Maggie that I know? Why hasn't she told me herself?"

"She doesn't know, right? You never met each other before now and Greg didn't tell her anything about you other than your first name—Joe."

"Right. But now that I know, I feel like I'm going to explode until I tell her. I've been thinking seriously about … I really feel like we were meant to be together."

Skye clapped her hands. "Oh wow! This is *wonderful*. Isn't this wonderful, Gabe?"

"Well, my darling, since I just got here, and I haven't met Maggie or Harper I'll just have to take your word for it." He chuckled.

Gabe shook Kane's hand. "Congratulations, Kane. I'm happy for you. Not exactly handing out cigars at the maternity nursery window, but joyful nonetheless."

"Thanks." Kane warmed more and more to the notion of becoming Harper's dad…and Maggie's husband. "I think I'm kind of thrilled."

"Thank you, Sacred Source," Skye said. "I was scared to death to hit you with this. I'm proud of you, Kane."

He ruffled Scarlet's downy soft hair. "I hope Maggie is as thrilled as I am. You guys want to stay for lunch?"

"Nah. Come on, my little darlings. Let's go home and do some coloring," Skye said.

Kane saw them out and then leaned his back against the front door, his future unfolding in his mind. He wanted to offer Maggie and Harper his home, his life. Maybe he could suggest that they stay with him rather than at the inn. He had more than enough guest suites in the house. Kane could spend uninterrupted time with them and ease into everyday fatherhood, decorate the house together for Christmas, enjoy quiet nights with Maggie by the fire.

He was in love with her—that fact was as unexpected for Kane as the news he had just received.

After Christmas he might go to Chicago, too. Whatever Maggie wanted. He glanced down at the Santa bag and grinned. "Let's see what your cousin, Skye, chose for your daddy to give you, Harper."

Chapter 17

Kane spent a sleepless night sitting at his piano staring out the window at the moonlit waves. The weight of Skye's revelation played heavily on his mind. He was a father and with that came a great responsibility. Was he up to the task? Would Maggie even let him try?

He needed to talk with Mom. Imagine her excitement learning that she had another grandchild…suddenly, out of the blue. No. This wasn't something he could tell her over the phone. So, when the sky brightened and turned scarlet, Kane left the studio, stepped out onto his deck, and peered down the beach off to his left. When he spotted his aunt taking her sunrise beach walk, he set off jogging to meet her.

"Here you are," Kay said. "Good morning." She gave him a hug.

"You were expecting me?"

"I was." She set in motion, and he fell in step with her.

"Did Skye tell you?"

"No, I haven't talked with Skye. She'd never break a confidence."

His intuition went into overdrive. "How long have you known that Harper is my daughter?" he said, not even trying to suppress the accusatory tone in his voice.

"Not long. Please don't be angry with me. As you know each year someone comes to the inn during the holidays for the first time and feels compelled to make a Christmas wish in a bottle. Sometimes I receive a vision of the guest beforehand, sometimes not. I wasn't thrilled when *In The Know* contacted me and asked if they could send a journalist here assuming that news of wishes come true had somehow become public. My first instinct was to say no, but deep down I knew that this was the Sacred Source's doing. As they say, the rest is history. I looked into Harper's eyes, and I just knew she was yours."

"But you didn't say anything? How could you have kept this from me, Aunt Kay?"

"I'm so sorry if I hurt you. If there is one thing I have learned over the years, I can't interfere with the Sacred Source. Everything will always be revealed in its own time."

"I don't know what to do." He scrubbed his face with his hand, his eyes gritty from lack of sleep.

"Of course you do." She halted and placed her hand on his chest. "What is your heart telling you to do?"

"Honestly, my heart tells me that Maggie is the one for me. I've thought seriously about proposing to her even before I found out about Harper."

Kay's lovely face lit with her wide smile reminding him so much of his mother. "Well, it seems to me you have your answer. You don't need advice."

"You don't think it's crazy for me to propose to Maggie after knowing her such a short time?"

Kay barked a laugh. "Crazy? Honey, this family's middle name is crazy. Seriously though, I met your uncle and that night I told my sisters that I was going to marry him. If he had asked me that first day, I would have said yes. Sometimes you just know."

Kane nodded. He did know.

"Thank you," he said, glad that he had sought Aunt Kay's opinion. He bent and kissed her cheek. "I have to run. I have some arrangements to make."

"Make your plans then come for breakfast."

"I will."

Kane sprinted back home, showered, dressed, and then spent the next hour planning. There was just one more phone call to make.

"Hey, Ty," Kane said when his brother picked up.

"Hey, bro. What do you need?"

No need to waste words. Kane and Ty shared a twin bond like no other. "I booked a private jet out of Midway tomorrow morning. Could you get Nana's ring out of my safe and bring it to me?"

"Sure. What time does my flight leave?"

"That's it? No questions?"

"Come on, Kane. How many times have you dropped everything to help me out? It's my turn."

"Thanks, Ty. This is really important to me. And one more favor—could you keep this to yourself and not tell Mom just yet?"

"My lips are sealed."

"I'll text you the flight info. Thanks again. I love you."

"Don't get all sappy on me."

He burst out laughing, delighted that Ty made it easy for this part of his plan to fall into place.

"Oh...and Kane? Congrats. Love you too." His brother disconnected.

****

Kane bounded up the deck stairs and entered the inn's kitchen through the sliding doors. "Something smells delicious," he said, trying to nab a sugary-cinnamon crumb off the coffee cake which Aunt Kay took out of the oven.

Aunt Kay shooed him away. "Wait until it cools." She winked at him. "You might want to go help your uncle at the front desk in the meantime."

"Of course." He'd never refuse assisting his family if he was able, but why would Uncle Mike need his help with reception duties?

When he encountered Maggie hanging over the front desk while his uncle spoke on the phone, he suspected that Aunt Kay might have had a hand in whatever caused the scowl on Maggie's face.

"Everything OK?" he said sensing from her tense posture and serious expression how she'd respond.

"Not really."

"What's the matter?"

"When we checked in originally, Kay said the reservation was made with a departure date of January 3rd. She said she fixed it when I told her we planned to check out the day after Christmas. Somehow, there was a computer glitch, and our room was double-booked. It looks like I have to check out today. I can't believe this."

"No luck at the Travelodge." Mike shook his head as he ran his finger down a list on a piece of paper in front of him. "I'm so sorry. Other than the summer peak season, Christmas and New Year are the busiest weeks here."

Kane offered no solution until Mike tried and failed to make the reservation at another local hotel and Maggie's face fell.

"I have a suggestion," he said.

"Really? What?" Maggie said between her teeth.

"Come stay at my house."

"We can't do that, Kane. Thank you for offering, though."

"Why not?"

"We've already imposed enough using your music studio."

"It's not an imposition. Think of this; Harper would be able to practice whenever she wants. We'll be able to rehearse for the concert whenever we want. If you have to go home today, Harper won't even be here for the concert."

"I don't know…"

"You haven't even seen the other wing of my house. There's a master bedroom which I built for when my parents visit, a kids' room with three beds, for when children in my family visit, a large den with a flat screen television and the most comfortable couch I have ever sat on and most importantly, I want you to," he said hoping he had convinced her. "Please," he added.

"Wow, Kane. If you really don't mind. This is wonderful. I don't know how to thank you."

Kane beamed at her. "Tell Harper we'll have sleep overs and watch movies and eat popcorn and junk food and have a pillow fight."

"When did you turn into a five-year-old girl?" she teased. "Seriously, it sounds like fun."

"I'm going to raid the kitchen for a hunk of coffee cake. Let me know when you're packed, and I'll take your suitcases to your car."

"I have an appointment later this afternoon to interview one of the candy bomber volunteers."

"We can get you all settled in beforehand. Maybe Harper and I will run some errands while you work. We could pick up dinner and meet you back at the house. How does that sound?"

"It sounds perfect."

Kane drifted into the kitchen. A generous piece of cake was plated on the countertop. He sat down on a stool and forked up a mouthwatering bite. Chewing contentedly, he pulled his phone out of his pocket and sent a text to Skye.

—*Did you buy a Christmas tree for me yet?*—

Three dots appeared followed by the response.

—*No, sorry. I haven't had time.*—

—*No problem. I'll do it myself today. Lu*—

—*That's the spirit! Lu 2*—

"Would you like pizza for dinner?" Kane said.

Harper sat in the back seat of his truck, gazing at him in her reflection in the rearview mirror. "I love pizza."

"What's your favorite?"

"Sausage and cheese and sometimes pepperoni. I even like peppers and onions. But *no* mushrooms."

"Got it, no mushrooms. I don't like mushrooms either."

He connected the Bluetooth call and placed their order with Slice Pizza. Next on his list, was a visit to the Christmas store. Kane didn't own a single Christmas decoration and that wouldn't do for what he had in mind.

"I don't have a Christmas tree and now that you and your mom are staying with me, I think I better buy one to decorate so Santa knows to stop at my house for you."

"Do you have stockings to hang?"

"I don't."

"We have to have stockings, too," she said, the little expert.

"I'm glad you're with me. You know more about

Christmas decorating than I do."

"Grandpa lets me help decorate the tree. He says I'm a good helper."

Her grandfather was right. Harper took charge scoping out the best ornaments as Kane followed her through the winding aisles filling a shopping basket. She chose a pink velvet stocking with the letter H embroidered on it.

"May I have this?"

"Of course you can."

She placed the find carefully on top of the ornaments in the basket.

"Do they have one with an M and a K?" Kane helped her search through the stockings in the display.

"Found an M for Mom and Maggie." Kane held up the matching pink stocking triumphantly.

"Oh no." Harper hung her hands at her sides in defeat. "The only K stocking is pink. No blue for a boy."

"No problem. Pink is fine with me. Anyway, I like that we'll match."

Next year we'll buy one with a D on it.

Done with picking out decorations, they headed to the Christmas tree display in the rear of the store.

"We have a fake tree with the lights already on it. Mommy says it's so much easier to put up. And no needles falling off."

"That works for me. Pre-lit and artificial it is." Kane found a store assistant and asked him to bring the boxed, ten-foot, "easy set up" model to the register.

He stowed the first Christmas décor purchases of his adult life in the truck and then drove to Slice Pizza Restaurant for the four pies, salad, and garlic knots that he had ordered.

Harper eyed the stack of boxes in Kane's arms. "That's a lot of food."

"You can never have enough pizza. Right?"

"Yes!" she crowed.

At home, Harper held the door open for him. "Honey, we're home," he sang out.

"That's a lot of food." Maggie cleared room to set the meal on the kitchen counter.

"You can never have enough pizza," Harper said straight-faced and little-girl wise.

His daughter was a quick study.

Their meal reminded him of family dinners at home: good food, laughter and sharing events of the day. Increasingly Kane thought of Harper and Maggie as his family.

When they unanimously declared there wasn't room for another bite, Kane volunteered to deal with the dishes and to put leftovers away. "Why don't you ladies change into pajamas or whatever's comfortable for movie watching and I'll meet you in the den."

"Can we please watch *White Christmas*?" Harper said.

"Of course we can. I'll queue it up when I'm done in the kitchen."

Kane loaded the dishwasher, cleaned the counter, and then changed his clothes in his bedroom. He opted to wear loose-fitting sweatpants and a soft hoodie. He grabbed his and Maggie's wine glasses from dinner, the open bottle of wine and a bottle of water for Harper and placed them on the coffee table in front of the flat screen television.

He searched Harper's movie, added it to "Up Next", and then settled into a corner of the sectional. Fifteen minutes passed before Maggie padded barefoot into the room.

"Harper stretched out on my bed while I was changing and fell instantly asleep. I didn't want to wake her, so I carried her to her room, and she stayed fast asleep. I guess our slumber party will have to wait until tomorrow night."

"Not necessarily." He patted the cushion next to him and Maggie sat down close to his side. "We can have our own party."

He dipped a finger into his wine glass, traced her lips with wine and then kissed her softly.

She sighed when he ended the kiss and snuggled closer to him. He wrapped an arm around her, feeling possessive and certain that he wanted to end every day like that, holding her near.

Maggie rested her head against his shoulder. "This is very nice. Thank you for letting us stay with you."

"Thank you for agreeing to stay with me. Would you like some wine?"

"No thank you. I'm so comfortable. I could stay here forever." She covered a yawn with her hand. "I'm sorry; it's been a long day."

"Still want to watch *White Christmas*, or something else?"

"Anything is fine."

He stuck with Harper's choice and started the movie because he fondly remembered his mother and aunts singing the sister, sister lyrics on the top of their lungs. In minutes Maggie went lax against his side and her breathing came in soft little purrs. Kane didn't wake her, enjoying the quiet intimacy of ending the day with his soulmate.

Kane had no doubt that he had found what he had searched for in Maggie. He needed to tell her that Harper was their daughter. But first, he had to tell her that he had fallen in love with her before he learned about Harper.

Tomorrow, he thought, gently moving away from Maggie to lower her down on her side. He scooched off the couch, lifted her legs so that she stretched out in slumber, covered her with a blanket, kissed her crown gently and then lay down on the couch on his side molding his body along hers and drawing her into the cradle of his arms.

****

She drifted into the kitchen at five a.m. as he was setting the coffee maker to brew. "Good morning. I'm sorry I fell asleep on you."

"Literally. I slept on the couch holding you in my arms all night. I never realized just how comfortable that sectional is."

A pretty blush pinkened her cheeks as she raised a hand to her hair. "You held me…"

"I hope I didn't wake you just now. I have a meeting today and I have to leave in a few minutes. I shouldn't be too late. I'll bring dinner."

"You don't have to do that. I'll make dinner for you."

"You can cook?"

"I didn't say it would taste good."

"Thankfully there's plenty of left over pizza." He dodged the swat that she aimed at his arm.

"I'll bring in the tree and the decorations Harper and I bought yesterday. Want to decorate together after dinner?"

"Sure. That sounds like fun."

"See you later then." He pulled her against his chest and kissed her goodbye thoroughly.

Releasing her, he flashed her a grin. "I assume you don't want me to tell anyone that I slept with you last night."

"You are impossible." She wadded up a dishtowel and threw it at him.

He caught the cloth on the fly and left the room. It took him a couple minutes to stop laughing.

Chapter 18

"Want to grab a beer while they refuel your plane?" Kane said.

Ty grinned at him. "I had a sandwich and two beers in flight. But I wouldn't mind another short one."

He sat on a stool at the small bar in the private terminal. "Not too shabby flying in a private jet. Thanks for the classy ride, Kane."

"Least I could do. Thanks for spending your day flying back and forth from Chicago for me, no questions asked." Kane joined his brother and ordered two beers on tap.

The bartender did a double-take eyeing his customers. The twins were accustomed to the reaction. Even though Ty's hair was cut shorter than Kane's and he tended to dress more fashionably, favoring tailored pants, fitted white tee shirts and designer blazers over Kane's black jeans and POLOs, the men were physically identical.

Kane opened the small jewelry box and inspected the heirloom engagement ring. The three-carat, round cut, emerald surrounded by diamond encrusted fillagree sparkled in the overhead light. He snapped the box shut and set it on the bar, satisfied that the ring he intended to give Maggie was worthy of her.

Ty raised his mug and gulped some beer. "Want to fill me in what's going on?"

"Yeah, I think I do, but bear with me. It's a lot." Kane took a sip of beer calculating where to begin. He put the mug down. "First of all, as you've probably surmised, I've found the woman I want to marry."

"Well, yeah. And as I said, congrats. But why the secrecy with Ma?"

"I really don't mean to be secretive. But it's a complicated situation. Not only is Maggie—that's her name, Maggie Larsen—the woman I want to marry, she's also the mother of my child."

Ty's eyes widened to saucers. "Hold on. You fathered a kid since you moved to OBX? How is that possible? You've only been here a few weeks."

"No, no. Harper—that's my daughter's name—is five years old."

"And Maggie just told you about this recently? Because you sure as hell haven't said a word about it in the last five years."

"Maggie doesn't know I'm Harper's father. I told you it's complicated."

He gave an exaggerated huff. "You can say that again. Truthfully, you lost me, Kane."

"Remember when I donated sperm for Greg Erikson, my undergrad and grad school roommate, because of his infertility?"

"O…kay. Yeah, I remember. So, Maggie is Greg's widow?"

"No. His sister-in-law. Greg married Maggie's sister, Eileen, who couldn't have children, either. Cancer, like Greg. Eileen asked Maggie to donate eggs and Maggie agreed to both be a donor and a surrogate for their child. Greg and Eileen died together in the plane crash when Maggie was almost nine months pregnant.

She has raised Harper alone for five years. She doesn't know that I'm her daughter's biological father. And I just learned about it. Maggie is a journalist doing a story on the inn. She and Harper checked in ten days ago."

Ty nodded, staring down at his drink. He turned his head and trained his gaze directly into Kane's eyes. "Look, Kane. I think you might be making a mistake here. I get that these are probably the most unusual circumstances you've ever faced, and you want to do the right thing. But marriage? You just met Maggie? Are you thinking clearly? I don't want to crush your plan, but isn't this kind of a far-out noble gesture?"

"I fell in love with Maggie before I learned that I'm Harper's biological father. And when I asked for Aunt Kay's opinion, she told me that she fell in love with Uncle Mike the first day she met him."

"Whoa, Aunt Kay is involved? And you haven't told Mom? She's going to kill you."

Kane burst out laughing. "I better call her before I propose. How do you think she'll take it?"

"Knowing Ma, she'll be thrilled for you. Maybe lead with, 'I fell in love at first sight, and oh, by the way, she has a daughter and I'm her dad!' Gees. Just promise me you know what you're doing."

"Never been more certain in my life."

"That's good enough for me." Ty finished off his beer, rose to his feet, and extended his right hand toward Kane.

He rose off the stool and accepted the handshake, and then pulled Ty into a man-hug.

"You'll pick up the tab, right, bro?" Ty said in motion toward the door leading out to the tarmac.

"Least I could do." Kane pulled out his wallet and

waved goodbye to his brother.

****

Kane made a stop at the store to pick up wrapping paper, ribbon, and a shirt box to camouflage Maggie's ring box before he returned home. Stepping into his foyer he was greeted with the savory, oniony smells of cooking. Before he sought out the source of the tantalizing aroma, and undoubtedly Maggie, the cook, he stowed her gift and the wrapping paper in his bedroom where he had hidden the Santa sack of presents Skye had picked out for him to give Harper.

He strode into the kitchen. "Something smells good and I'm starving."

Maggie turned away from the stove, wooden spoon in hand. His heart skipped a beat at the sight of her. She looked lovely dressed in a simple outfit of jeans and a pine green sweater covered in embroidered candy canes wearing her long blonde hair held up in back with a banana clip. Loose tendrils framed her porcelain face, and she wore just enough makeup to highlight her full lips and round lawn-green eyes.

"It's my version of turkey chili," she said.

"I love chili. When do we eat?"

"If you can drag Harper away from the piano, we can eat now. Don't get too excited. This chili doesn't have *any* chili powder or pepper in it. Harper can't stand spicy food."

"Not chili, chili. Got it."

"But…. I bought some diced pepperoncini. That's how I spice it up a bit. Tons of shredded, sharp cheddar cheese and the pepperoncini on top. I also put the chili over pasta."

"This sounds good. I'll set the table and then I'll

round up Harper."

****

After they ate dinner, Kane declared that he had enjoyed the meal. Harper had scarfed hers down knowing the treat they had in store for dessert. At least Maggie hoped that it tasted like a treat.

Maggie took tin foil off of the plate of Christmas sugar cookies that she and Harper had baked and decorated that morning. She placed the platter of iced snowmen, Christmas trees, Santa hats and candy canes in the center of the table. She was probably insane to make cookies when Kane's mother was the founder of an internationally famous cookie company and his aunt baked delectable baked goods, but Harper had always loved her cookies.

"What's this?"

"We made them," Harper said. "How many can I have?"

"How about one at a time and we'll talk," Maggie said, picking up a cookie and nibbling on it while she watched Kane.

Since he ate four cookies in short order, she figured he either loved her attempt at baking or was the politest faker ever. Harper kept pace with Kane and most likely would have kept going if Maggie hadn't insisted that she had eaten enough.

Maggie loved Christmas—even the work involved with putting up a tree and decorating their condo with sparkly lights. She missed doing that with her parents and Harper that year. But trimming Kane's tree with him more than made up for missing out on decorating at home.

Instrumental Christmas carols played throughout

the house. He lifted Harper up so that she could place the star on the top of the tree and hang ornaments on the highest boughs. Maggie loved the way he related to Harper and the hero worship that shone in her daughter's eyes relating to Kane. Maggie and Harper had taken up temporary residence in his home with ease. He made them feel so welcome…as if they belonged there…with him. She had even enjoyed cooking dinner that night using his dream-kitchen appliances and shiny pots and pans and could envision cooking for him or with him every day and spending every night in his arms.

She loved Kane's generosity, his soul stirring, steamy kisses, his incredible talent, his superb role modeling for Harper, his gorgeous face, his sexy muscles. Maggie loved everything about Kane. With the end of their stay on Outer Banks looming, she resolved to not wait any longer than after Harper went to bed to tell him that she was in love with him, whether he felt the same way about her or not.

Reading to Harper at bedtime was a cherished tradition for Maggie knowing that in a few years, her daughter would more than likely prefer reading by herself. But that night, Maggie had to restrain herself from rushing the story in her eagerness to talk to Kane. When she finally kissed her little girl good night, she hurried to the den to be with him.

Kane had kindled a fire and lazed on the sofa facing the hearth, his legs propped up on the coffee table.

"Hey." He lowered his feet to the floor. "Come sit."

She sat down next to him and took the glass of wine he offered her. Clinking glasses they toasted, "Cheers," and took sips. Maggie set her glass on the table and gazed into Kane's soft blue eyes, longing to tell him everything about her, about Harper, about how she felt about him and what it could mean if he loved her, too.

Maggie was a mother above all things. First things first. "I want to tell you the story of Harper's conception and birth. But I don't want you to get upset if I cry."

He touched her knee gently. "No need, sweetheart. Skye told me about your sister and brother-in-law. She told me everything."

"*What?*" She frowned, shocked that Skye would gossip about something so personal. "I can't believe she'd take it upon herself to—"

"Don't be mad," he interjected. "She told me because she knows I'm crazy in love with you and—"

"You're crazy in love with me?" she interrupted him, her heart winging with joy. "Oh Kane, I'm in love with you, too."

He wrapped his arms around her whispering in her hair, "Darling, that makes me the happiest man alive, but there's more I want to say." Kane released the hug and stared straight ahead at the fire. "I studied at the Yale School of Music for my graduate degree."

"Wow. That doesn't surprise me knowing how hard it is to get accepted there. My brother-in-law, Greg Erikson, received his Masters' degree from the Yale School of Music, too."

"Yes." He continued to gaze at the fire. "I knew Greg very well. He was my roommate in undergrad and graduate school."

"I…" Her head swam. "How can that be? You must have confused him with someone else. Greg's roommate's name was Joe."

"I know." Kane turned his head toward her. His penetrating gaze unnerved her. He took hold of both of her hands. "Joseph is my middle name. Remember how I told you I detested my first name. When I was a kid, I insisted that everybody call me Joe instead of Hurrikane. It stuck until I was about twenty-five."

His words sliced through her, and her heart froze in her chest. "You mean…you are…" She could hardly breathe.

"We were as close as brothers." He clasped her hands tighter. "When he asked me to donate sperm, I didn't hesitate for a second. Skye figured out that I'm Harper's father when you told her the story."

She yanked her hands away while her thoughts fractured, and emotions whirled like a cyclone. "I can't…I'm sorry, Kane. I need to think." She bolted up off the couch.

He gazed up at her. "Please, Maggie. I love you. And Harper. I fell in love with both of you before I knew any of this."

All she could think was that she had to be alone and somehow wrap her head around this.

"I do love you, Kane. I just need to sleep on this. We'll talk more in the morning. OK?"

Kane knit his brow, but he stayed seated and didn't make the first move to stop her. "Of course. Good night, sweetheart. If you need anything during the night, promise you'll wake me?"

"Yes. Sure. Good night, Kane."

She sped away from him shaken to the core. Did Kane tell her that he loved her because of some sense of duty or chivalry or to honor Greg's memory? Harper was hers. Alone. Did she want to share her just because of biology?

In the few minutes it took to flee to her guest room

and close the door behind her, she made up her mind. She'd pack their things and she and Harper would leave, hopefully before Kane awakened the next morning.

A half hour later she crawled into bed and cried herself to sleep.

Chapter 19

Maggie lugged their suitcases down the stairs to the foyer one at a time in her stocking feet, tiptoed back upstairs to put on shoes and then retraced her steps. The hinges squeaked when she opened the front door, freezing her to the spot. She strained to hear any evidence that she had awakened Kane, but the house remained quiet.

She loaded the trunk of the rental car and hurried back upstairs.

"Time to get up, sweetie," she said, gently nudging awake her deeply sleeping daughter.

"Huh?" Harper blinked several times. "It's still dark outside."

"I know. But we have to get going. You can sleep in the car."

Maggie helped Harper dress—more like dressing a ragdoll—and then ushered her out of the house. Harper was asleep in the backseat before Maggie pulled the car onto the bypass.

She navigated the blessedly light traffic, her eyes burning and her nose stuffy from crying off and on all night. When she did manage some fitful sleep, she had awful dreams about Kane taking Harper away from her. Her hands trembled on the steering wheel as she recalled the nightmares.

She was close to the airport when the traffic started

to build, a welcome bit of good fortune since she was cutting close the time before her flight's scheduled departure. Maggie checked their bags to O'Hare after dropping off the rental car, breezed through security and arrived at their gate just as the flight was boarding.

Harper hadn't spoken since leaving the house. But as Maggie buckled her into the seat on the plane, her eyes filled with tears.

"Aw, sweetie. Why are you crying?"

"Because we're going home. I don't understand why we left."

"Something came up at work. I'm so sorry to upset you."

"But what about the concert?" Her voice caught. "Kane needs me."

"If I can get everything straightened out with work in time, maybe we can go back," she lied, something she usually avoided doing where Harper was concerned.

Maggie hoped that anticipating Santa's arrival would make Harper forget about the concert—and forget about Kane.

The plane soared skyward just as the sun rose. The heavens were aflame with streaks of red, magenta, and orange reminding Maggie of the gorgeous dawns at the inn. A flight attendant brought coffee and juice. Maggie let Harper play games on her iPad without restriction. Her heart breaking that she had felt forced to flee, Maggie sipped coffee and tried to squelch memories of her stay on Outer Banks.

She emerged from the jet bridge at O'Hare. A male voice hollered, "Maggie! Over here!"

Her heart flipflopped and her hands started trembling again. Had Kane somehow followed them?

She frantically searched the faces of passersby torn between wanting to escape Kane and running into his arms.

She spotted her boss, Nick Carter, at the next gate over waving his arms overhead.

Clasping Harper's hand, she bustled over to greet him. "Hi, Nick. What are you doing here?"

"Last minute decision when the in-laws called. Sloan thought they sounded lonely on the phone, so we're on our way to California to surprise them for Christmas."

"Where are Sloan and the girls?"

"Shopping, of course, before they get on the plane. But aren't you on assignment until after Christmas? I haven't seen your article yet."

"Something came up and we had to come home a few days early. I have everything I need to submit my piece by the deadline."

"That's great." He glanced at his watch. "I better round up the girls; boarding will start soon."

He stooped down and gave Harper a hug. "Merry Christmas. Harper."

Rising to hug Maggie, he said, "And Merry Christmas to you, Maggie. See you next year."

"Have a wonderful time."

Maggie headed towards the baggage claim area, Harper in tow, halting as they turned onto the main concourse. Huge red bows topped sky-high garlands trimmed with hundreds of white lights. The distinctive globe which hung from the center of the domed ceiling sparkled with lights and beautiful, illuminated doves overhead amazed.

Maggie used her phone to snap a photo—one of

many she had taken of O'Hare's Christmas finery over the years. The decorations had always filled Maggie with joy when she traveled during the holidays—festive sendoffs and beautiful welcomes home.

Maggie ordered an Uber after she heaved their bags off of the conveyor belt. Frigid air outside had them shivering on the curb waiting for their car to arrive. Harper huddled next to Maggie without making a peep during the ride home.

The scent of pine from the diffuser she had left on a shelf in her condo afforded a tiny bit of Christmas-like cheer in their undecorated home. Harper hung her coat on a peg next to the door and then wheeled her suitcase into the laundry room and Maggie followed suit.

The laundry could wait until after she took a shower and changed into comfortable clothes. Emerging into the living room fifteen minutes later feeling revived and comfortable, Maggie encountered Harper with her nose pressed to the window mesmerized by newly falling snow. She joined her at the window bank content to return to their cocoon—just the two of them, living the life that Maggie had built for her and her daughter out of the tragedy of losing her sister.

"Are we going back for the concert now that Mr. Carter is going on vacation?" The hopeful innocence shining in Harper's eyes shattered Maggie's sense of peace.

"Um, we'll see. With my boss on vacation, they may need me even more at the office," she improvised.

The sad expression on Harper's face twisted Maggie in knots. "I better start the laundry and I have work to do. When I'm done, I'll make hot chocolate for us, and we can cuddle and watch the snow fall."

Her sweet girl nodded without complaint.

She opened the garment bag on the laundry room floor first—a mistake. Their dresses for the concert were the first two items on top. Tears brimmed in Maggie's eyes as she hung the dresses in her bedroom closet.

Kane was the first man she had loved in a long time—maybe the first man she had ever truly loved. And she had told him she loved him unknowingly exposing herself and Harper to threatening heartbreak.

Why hadn't she told Harper that they decidedly were not going back to the Outer Banks?

Maggie had checked her phone repeatedly and he hadn't even tried to contact her. Had she left the door open to bring Harper back to the Outer Banks hoping Kane might beg her to return?

He said he's crazy in love with me. Is he? Or does he want to use me to get close to Harper?

She hardly knew him. How could she trust him? Her head spun as confusion mounted.

At least she could control her work, so she sat at the computer in her home office and reviewed her emails. She had completed her article except for some details about the candy bomber event. Happy that the volunteer she had interviewed had followed up with promised photos, Maggie opened the email attachments consecutively and gasped at a shot of Kane and Harper joyfully gazing skyward at the approaching "bomber". They looked so comfortable together…like a loving father and daughter. The next photo was a closeup of Kane and Maggie at the event with eyes just for each other, Harper a blurry figure in the background.

Maggie studied the adoring expression on Kane's face—for her. He hadn't known about Harper at the time the photo was taken. "What am I doing here, Kane, without you?"

"What did you say, Mommy?" Harper called out.

"Nothing, sweetie. Just talking to myself."

She opened the internet browser and searched for a flight to Norfolk from O'Hare on Christmas Eve day, curious if returning was at all possible. There was an early morning flight with two first class tickets left. Without hesitating she put the itinerary on a twenty-four-hour hold, turned off her computer and drifted into the kitchen to make hot chocolate.

The fridge was essentially bare, so their meal was Harper's favorite, breakfast for dinner—pancakes made from a box mix with water drenched with maple syrup. They ate in front of the television on a blanket on the floor, picnic style.

Harper fell asleep minutes after brushing her teeth and saying her prayers. Maggie poured a glass of wine and checked her email and text messages. Still no contact from Kane. Relief and crushing disappointment continued emotional warfare inside Maggie.

She placed her wine glass on the lamp table next to her bed, turned on the television in her room, slipped under the covers and scooted up to sit leaning against the headboard surfing channels. Nothing on TV held her interest. She opened a book instead. After she read the same page five times, she chugged the rest of her wine and turned off the light.

When she was on the brink of sleep she thought she heard a soft voice say, "This is not where the story ends."

Too groggy to decipher the waking dream, Maggie fell deeply asleep.

****

Kane had wanted to follow Maggie when she fled the family room last night, but he had forced himself to give her the time she needed to process the fact that he was Harper's father. He was shocked, too. Even so, that they had found each other and had fallen in love seemed miraculous to him.

The house was quiet when he gave up staring at the ceiling for hours instead of sleeping. He drifted into the kitchen to fix breakfast for three while his thoughts centered around his best course of action. Should he wait until Christmas Day as planned to propose? Maybe he should drop down onto one knee that morning as soon as Maggie appeared in his kitchen?

Yes. Today. He put a couple of waffles into the toaster oven and set bacon strips sizzling in a skillet before leaving the room to retrieve her engagement ring. Kane placed the velvet box on the kitchen counter and finished cooking breakfast.

After three cups of coffee and an hour of keeping the waffles and bacon warm, Kane ambled to the guest wing of the house to check on Maggie and Harper. Maggie's door was ajar.

Kane rapped lightly on the door. "Maggie? Are you up?"

No response.

He swung the door fully open and peered into her room. The bed was perfectly made. Kane bounded inside and checked the closet sensing even before he verified that he'd find it empty. He jogged down the hall. Harper's room, ditto. Opening the shutters on the window he gazed out at the driveway.

Gone.

They were gone. Kane could scarcely breathe,

feeling as empty as his guest rooms. He stomped back to the kitchen, turned off the warming oven and grabbed his phone off the counter. He almost flung the device in the garbage can. The battery was dead.

Why did she leave him without any explanation? He thought last night was the start of their new life together as a family. Was he delusional believing that she loved him as he loved her? How could he be so wrong? He had to find her, and he knew where he should start. Kane headed towards the inn.

The breakfast buffet was in full swing but the last thing on his mind was food. He forced smiles and greeted the guests milling around the counter and even chatted with a couple about the upcoming concert, all the while itching to consult with Aunt Kay.

She appeared in the doorway beckoning to him. He followed her out of the kitchen into the parlor at the front of the inn.

He slumped on the couch next to her. "Have you heard from Maggie?"

"Well no. Isn't she staying at your house?"

"Yes. Until this morning. She was gone when I checked on her and Harper after they didn't come to breakfast. I didn't hear them leave."

"Did you have a fight?"

"Not exactly. Last night she began to tell me the story of Harper's conception and I interrupted by telling her Skye had already given me the details. Maybe Maggie was miffed at her for breaking a confidence, but I defended Skye explaining why she came to me with the information. Skye knows I'm in love with Maggie. I told Maggie I love her and that I was Greg's sperm donor."

"All right…and then what happened? How did she

take it?"

"It was a lot for her to handle. She couldn't get away from me fast enough, honestly. I wanted her to continue talking about it, but she said she needed some time to think in her room, and we'd talk in the morning—today. She went to her bedroom and that's the last time I saw her."

Kane was too agitated to sit still. He rose to his feet and paced back and forth. "Do you have any idea where they are?"

Kay closed her eyes and sat perfectly still. Kane respected his aunt's gift and held his breath hoping that a vision would come.

"She's back in her home," Kay said. "I saw clearly."

He heaved a sigh. "Thanks. I'm on my way."

She clutched his arm when he bent to kiss her goodbye. "You shouldn't follow her, Kane. Let her be for now. I see that she'll come back to you, but she must make this decision on her own. You can't force this."

He sank back down onto the couch. "I can't stay here and do nothing."

"I know it's hard for you, dear. And I don't like to tell you what to do. But if you love her, you'll wait for her. This is not where the story ends."

Chapter 20

Kane plugged his phone into the charger on his kitchen island and then stood in the middle of the room aimless and frustrated with the waiting game his aunt had recommended. He wanted to inundate Maggie with a flurry of texts, phone calls—send her flowers, appear at her door, beg her to be with him.

Anything to alleviate this vacuum of longing.

If she did come back, true to Aunt Kay's prediction, would she reject his proposal? He sat down hard on a counter stool mulling over that possibility. What would he do if she returned just to tell him that she never wanted to see him again?

"If you love her, you'll wait for her," Aunt Kay had said.

I do. And I guess I just have to leave this in the hands of the Sacred Source. No other choice.

He shoved off the stool bound for his studio hoping to lose himself in his music for a while. Kane took a few steps toward the kitchen doorway. His phone bleated and buzzed along the surface of the island. He pounced on it and connected the call, the charger wire dangling by his ear.

"Maggie? Hi."

"Uh, sorry, Kane. It's Ty."

His stomach sank. "I was hoping…never mind. What's up?"

Ty belly laughed. "I'm not the one proposing marriage. What's up with *you*? I called to see how the proposal went. By the way, did you call Ma yet?"

Kane rubbed his eyes. "Uh…no I haven't called her yet. Haven't proposed yet, either."

"Oh, OK. I forgot to ask you when you were going to pop the question. When *are* you going to ask her? Have you figured out some romantic way to go about this? Underneath the mistletoe? Put the ring in a glass of champagne toasting on New Year's Eve? Are you going to get down on one knee? Ask her father for her hand in marriage?"

He hadn't thought of that. Would Maggie expect him to follow that old fashioned tradition? Kane huffed a laugh at his brother's prying despite the depressing reality of his abandonment.

"Maggie left me sometime between last evening and this morning after I told her that I'm the college roommate sperm donor."

"Oh boy. I take it, it didn't go well?"

"Understatement. According to Aunt Kay, she's back home in Chicago as we speak."

"Aunt Kay had a vision?"

"She did. After I begged her to try when I woke up and found Maggie gone."

"Wait. Chicago? She lives here?"

"Yeah. River North."

"Small world! Want me to go over there and introduce myself. I'll beg for her mercy on your behalf. I can be charming for you."

For a split second, Kane almost agreed to send Ty to grovel at Maggie's feet as his emissary. Ty was charm personified. But he trusted his aunt and had no intention of defying the Sacred Source.

"Thanks, but I have to trust that she'll work through this on her own. Aunt Kay said she'll come back. Wish me luck," Kane said.

"You've got it. This was supposed to be a surprise, but we're all coming to OBX in time for the Christmas Eve concert and to celebrate Christmas together. Aunt Kay and Mom have cooked up the whole thing. Want me to come early and keep you company?"

Kane smiled. "No need, but thanks. I see you haven't changed since you were a kid. You could never keep a secret. Wait a minute…" Suspicion morphed into certainty. "You told Mom already about the proposal."

"Maybe…"

Kane burst out laughing. "I love you, bro. See you Christmas Eve."

The prospect of seeing his family buoyed his sagging spirits. Maybe Maggie would return for Christmas, too. He'd like nothing better than for her to meet his family. And if he was lucky, to introduce her as his fiancée. Surely, she wouldn't deprive Harper of performing in the concert whether she wanted to be with him or not. Would she? He hoped his aunt was right and that Maggie might give him a second chance.

Kane would turn to his music for solace. Although, how could he sit at one of the pianos in his studio and not sorely miss Harper dueling next to him?

****

Maggie sidled up to the spinet piano, coffee mug in hand. Harper had practiced all morning non-stop while Maggie had finalized her article.

"That's a pretty piece, sweetie."

"Thanks, Mommy." She kept playing without

skipping a note.

It wasn't lost on Maggie that Harper hadn't played a single Christmas song during the long stint at the piano.

"Why haven't you practiced your Christmas music, honey?"

She stopped playing and shrugged her shoulders. "I need Kane for that."

Harper trained doleful, crystalline blue eyes on her. A jolt of recognition quaked through Maggie. Her daughter had Kane's beautiful eyes. For that matter, Harper had his identical raven hair color, too. And his long piano fingers. She had Kane's complexion coloring…her father's features. Now Harper's musical talent from such an early age made perfect sense considering her genealogy. How had Maggie missed something so obvious?

Truly Harper didn't resemble Maggie at all—except in temperament. Maggie was grateful for Harper's patience and maturity beyond her years. She hadn't exhibited a bit of defiance despite her disappointment that Maggie had dragged her back home against her will. And kept her there, away from the fun and festivities of The Inn of the Three Butterflies and the sweet company of the famous composer who lived down the beach. No defiance from her daughter. Only sadness.

Harper needed Kane to play her joyful holiday songs. Maybe Maggie needed Kane, too.

She sat down on her sofa lost in thought as Harper resumed playing the piano. Eileen, her stunning, beloved sister, appeared in her mind's eye, smiling just like she had when she was happiest. She remembered Eileen's and Greg's joyful gratitude the night that she had agreed to help them become parents. And Eileen's huge smiles that came from planning for the baby's birth together, the OB visits, the tiny baby's image on ultrasounds. Maggie would never understand why the Lord chose to take her sister and brother-in-law away from her and the baby that they wanted with all their hearts. She wished she didn't have to live without her sister's love.

Maggie closed her eyes, happy that she could still envision Eileen's beautiful face. In her pine-scented room, memories of Christmases with her sister spooled in her mind like a much-loved video. Eileen was only twenty-two months older than Maggie, so they never had to overcome too wide an age gap divide between them. Sibling arguments? Sure. Especially when they were teens and hormones saturated.

But sibling rivalry was non-existent between her and Eileen. For years the gifts that they eagerly stripped of wrapping paper under the tree on Christmas morning were identical: dolls, stuffed animals, games, roller skates, ice skates—Santa apparently made their toys in twos.

She had loved to sing with Eileen. They worked out harmonies and caroled together seated on the floor beneath the Christmas tree shoulder-to-shoulder, their legs outstretched, their eyes sparkling with reflected fairy lights. In Maggie's memory, they had sounded almost professional.

They had loved to walk and talk together. During the winter holidays when darkness gathered early, they'd volunteer to walk the dog after dinner so that they could gawk at Christmas decorations and gaze through windows at decorated trees making up stories about the home lives they spied like peeping Toms.

One Christmas when Maggie was ten years old,

Aunt Pam, Mom's sister, and her family came to celebrate the holidays with them. Maggie and Eileen hero worshipped their athletic cousins Tim and Mark. Tim was two years older than Eileen and Mark was a year younger putting Maggie last in the hierarchy. But the best things about spending time with her then teenage older cousins were they didn't treat her like a baby know-nothing, and they defended her faithfully.

That Christmas was snowy and bitter cold. Maggie's family lived in a ranch house on a cul-de-sac of eight homes in the northwest suburbs of Chicago. Arlington Heights was a nice community with efficient services for their residents including frequent snow plowing of all the roads in town including their little street. What resulted that year were heaps of snow ringing the circular street that provided a fortress for epic snowball fights.

Defending Fernandez Place against all snowball-armed attackers on Christmas Day fell to Tim, Eileen, Mark, and Maggie. She was the only one of the foursome bundled into a snowsuit which was great for insulation from the cold and not so great for freedom of movement. Maggie couldn't run encased in the bulky padding, so Tim and Mark barricaded Maggie and Eileen behind their muscular bodies.

The boys developed a rhythm of parting so that Eileen and Maggie could fire off shots and then closing rank so the girls could take cover behind the boys. She and her sister were untouchable and always victorious when their cousins were around.

Her treasure trove of beautiful holiday memories of Eileen overflowed. She had shared only twenty-four Christmases with her sister—a quarter of which she was too young to remember.

Christmas Wish in a Bottle

The Christmas Eve a month after Eileen's successful cancer surgery blazed in Maggie's memory. Her little family was ebullient, ecstatic, and grateful to the core. How foolish to stop worrying that Eileen might die.

She loved her sister enormously, unconditionally and missed her more each day.

Maggie's thoughts turned to chatting with Kane about favorite Christmases past—puppies and surprises and family. He had a soft heart—a big heart.

Did Kane miss Greg, a man he described as like a brother to him? He must have felt similarly about Greg as she did about Eileen to agree to help him become a father. Granted, Kane's sacrifice didn't compare to Maggie's, but his intentions seemed as selfless.

Maybe she was wrong to run away before hearing him out? Maybe she was wrong not to trust him? Maybe she was wrong to prevent Harper from seeing him? Maybe she was wrong about everything.

Her article was done and submitted. The airline reservations were still on hold. Her parents were still sailing the seven seas and her daughter was obviously miserable about the situation.

She rose from her seat and drained her now cold coffee into the sink. Bending over her phone, Maggie opened the airline app and completed the purchase for the next day's flights.

"I'll be back in a few minutes," she sang out.

Harper abruptly quit playing Fur Elise for the umpteenth time. "Where are you going, Mommy?"

"Down the hall to the storage locker. I'll be right back."

Maggie grabbed her keyring out of a bowl on her kitchen counter, swung out the door and hurried down the hall. When she returned rolling two suitcases behind her, Harper's jaw dropped, and she popped up from the piano bench like a jack in the box.

"We're going back for the concert!" she screeched, grinning from ear to ear.

"We are. As soon as we wake up *really* early tomorrow."

Harper rushed straight at her and threw her arms around Maggie's waist. "Oh, thank you, Mommy! Can I go to bed now so tomorrow comes fast?"

She ruffled Harper's hair and then held on to her shoulders at arm's length smiling into her Kane-like eyes.

"That won't make morning come sooner, but we do have to go to sleep much earlier than normal. No time for a Christmas movie."

"That's OK. I'm so happy!" Harper's little body thrummed with excitement.

For a moment, Maggie faltered. Kane hadn't called to convince her to return or hadn't appeared magically at O'Hare Airport. Had she pushed him away completely? How in the world would they deal with explaining complicated biology to her kindergartner?

Eileen's smiling face flashed in her mind again. *This is where the story begins,* she seemed to say.

Maggie didn't care about the technicalities. The pall of loneliness and confusion lifted as she looked forward to a reunion with Kane.

Chapter 21

Kane debated calling. The last thing he wanted to do was wake her. Sure, he wanted to see his family for Christmas—if things had worked out differently with Maggie. But he was alone, feeling sorry for himself and he didn't want to bring his family down during the holidays. He jumped as his phone vibrated in his hand.
Maggie?
A quick glimpse at the caller ID disappointed him. But his brother's timing a call at nearly midnight the day before Christmas Eve was perfect, sparing his disturbing their mother.

Ty assured him that everything was fine with his family, but he had phoned sensing that something was bothering him. That mysterious twin connection in play.

Kane probably didn't need to explain his reasoning in asking Ty to cancel the holiday trip to the Outer Banks since his brother knew him as well as he knew himself. But he apologized anyway and promised to fly home on Christmas Day.

It meant a lot to Kane that Ty understood and that he would handle breaking the news to Mom. What meant even more were Ty's parting words before ending the call. "Kane, I know everything is going to work out with Maggie."

****

Maggie and Harper arrived at O'Hare at five a.m.,

one and a half hours before their scheduled boarding time. She had found a space in long term parking in minutes and had packed only a carry on.

Encountering the milling crowd and endless lines inside the terminal, she was delighted with her foresight in deciding not to pack their large suitcases the night before. She walked briskly to the end of the TSA Pre-Check queue that seemed to stretch half the length of the vast building, took her place in line, and checked her phone app for their flight status. The departure board to her left displayed several delayed and cancelled flights.

She expelled a sigh of relief. Her flight was still on time. Inching in line toward the security check-in booth, Maggie obsessively checked her watch. The flight attendant announced pre-boarding just as they breathlessly arrived at the gate—of course the farthest out from the main concourse. In minutes they proceeded to board the first-class passengers.

Her excitement over their perfect timing dissolved shortly after the plane pulled away from the gate. Although the passengers were free to move around the plane for the duration, the captain parked in a holding area waiting out a passing snowstorm. The jet was de-iced twice before the possibility that they might not leave Chicago at all struck Maggie. Even if the plane eventually took off, time was slipping away, and she had to figure in a two-hour drive after they landed in Norfolk.

The delay finally ended. It was too close to call whether they would arrive at the Mansion in time for the concert. She repeatedly sent positive thoughts out into the universe.

Harper studied sheet music instead of playing on an iPad, although Maggie had no doubt that she could play every song from memory.

She raised her eyes from the sheet music spread out in her lap and beamed at Maggie. "Thank you, Mommy for taking me back."

Maggie patted her leg. "I know how excited you are about playing in the concert."

"And my wish in my bottle, too. I can't wait until Christmas morning!"

"When did you make a wish, sweetie?"

"Mister Kane helped me."

"He did? That was nice of him."

Kane hadn't told her, but she wasn't surprised that he had extended the kindness to her girl… His girl, too, she thought with a start.

Maybe she could wrap a picture of a puppy and a note promising they'd find a dog to adopt when they returned home—if she could use a printer somewhere, nab a box and then, the materials to wrap the gift. It was going to be a long night.

The flight dragged for Maggie and the second the seat belt light extinguished, she popped up from her seat, grabbed her bag out of the overhead bin, took hold of Harper's hand, and made a beeline for the rental car desk once out of the jet bridge.

The line at the counter snaked like an amusement park attraction zigzag. She tapped her toe, helpless to do anything but shuffle forward in frustrating degrees until it was finally her turn.

Keys and rental car agreement in hand, she detoured to the rest room. She didn't want to forfeit travel time but decided that Harper needed to change clothes so that she was concert-ready the moment they arrived.

Harper donned her red velvet dress and white tights

decorated with candy canes. She switched her tennis shoes to Mary Janes while Maggie brushed her hair and then swept her dark curls back and fastened it with a red bow clip.

The clock on the dashboard read four thirty as Maggie steered out of the lot and her Waze App predicted ETA at six forty-five. Fifteen minutes to spare before the concert started. *Fingers crossed.*

****

Traffic started to build as the App directed Maggie onto Rte.168, the "fastest" route. She groaned. Nothing but brake lights up ahead and she came to a complete standstill at the toll booth. *Wonder what the slowest route is?*

The jam from a fender bender cleared quickly, however. By the time they zoomed over the Wright Memorial Bridge and turned onto Rte. 12, a straight shot to the Mansion, the revised ETA was 7:30.

All was not lost since Harper would perform at the end of the concert. She still had a chance to deliver her there in time.

But where the heck do I park for the shuttle?

Wasting no time, Maggie dialed Skye's number, weak with relief when she answered on the first ring.

"Merry Christmas, Maggie. I'm afraid I can't talk for long. The concert will start in a few minutes."

"I know. I hate to bother you, but I don't know where to park to get the shuttle."

"You're on the sandbar?" Skye shrieked. "Kane didn't say a word to me."

"He doesn't know. Harper wants to surprise him."

"Oh, he'll definitely be surprised. Hold on a sec."

"Gabe asked do you have a four-wheel drive car?"

"No. The rental car is a little economy model."

"Okay. In that case, Gabe said to keep driving through Corolla until you see the giant Wings store on your left. Pull into the parking lot and he'll come and get you."

"Oh no, I don't want to take him away from the concert."

"He already left. Trust me, he jumped at the excuse to miss some of the concert." Skye chuckled. "I have to go. The concert is starting. I'm so glad you're here."

Ten minutes later, Maggie parked the car, freshened her lipstick, and brushed her hair. Her lovely green satin dress remained packed in her suitcase, so she felt underdressed for the evening. Still, the black velvet slacks and red cashmere sweater she had chosen to wear on the plane were festive and dressy enough for the event, she hoped.

An F-150 truck topped with a flashing light bar roared down the road, turned into the parking lot, and parked next to their car.

A dark-haired man wearing a perfectly cut suit, white shirt and red tie climbed out of the truck and rounded the front bumper of Maggie's car. Her heart leaped because for a moment, she thought he was Kane. She tried not to be too disappointed when she realized it wasn't.

Maggie opened her car door and slipped out of her seat smiling up at the man. "You must be Gabe. It's a pleasure to meet you. I'm very fond of Skye and your daughters."

He smiled broadly reminding Maggie of Kane once more. "The pleasure is mine, Maggie."

Gabe shook Maggie's hand. "I've heard so much

about you that I feel like I already know you."

"Same here. Thank you for coming to get us." Maggie opened the back door, unlatched Harper's seatbelt, and hoisted her carry on off the back seat.

"No problem at all," Gabe said. "You must be Harper. Nice to finally meet you."

"Thank you," Harper said. "I like playing with the three little Esses."

He huffed a laugh, grabbing Maggie's suitcase in hand, led them to the truck, helped them to mount into the seats, and stowed Maggie's suitcase. Gabe jumped behind the wheel and then blazed out of the parking lot with red lights flashing in swirling reflections on the road. The cars ahead pulled over and let them pass.

"This is so cool." Harper said. "Everyone is letting us go."

"I borrowed my friend's truck. He's a fireman. My truck doesn't have these cool lights." He winked at Maggie.

Gabe drove the massive vehicle onto the beach and up along the service road at the back of the Mansion where he braked and slammed the gearshift into park. "We're here."

He lifted Harper out of the back seat while Maggie shoved open her door and climbed out of the truck.

Harper pointed towards the dark stretch of sand that they had just crossed. "Mommy, that's where Kane showed me the three horses I told you about."

The beautiful sound of voices raised in song swelled inside the vestibule of the Mansion. Gabe excused himself and went to join Skye and the triplets in the audience.

A woman holding a stack of programs hurried over

to them. "Harper, I'm so glad you were able to make it. Kane told me that something came up and you weren't coming."

The woman reached out her hand to greet Maggie. "I'm Mavis; you must be Harper's mom."

"Nice to meet you Mavis, I'm Maggie. I hope Harper hasn't missed her chance to play with Kane."

"She hasn't. I'll take you backstage. You're just in time."

Mavis led the way down a narrow corridor. She stopped outside a door and raised an index finger to her lips. Then she opened the door gingerly, beckoned them inside with a wave of her arm, handed Maggie a program, and closed the door softly, leaving them in the dimly lit wings of the stage.

Maggie spied Kane from behind. He was seated at a piano and wearing a black tuxedo. A second piano faced his—waiting for Harper to take her place.

Maggie checked the program Mavis had provided. "You're on after this song, honey. I'm so proud of you," she whispered.

Kane's deep voice sounded, sending shivers through Maggie. "There's a change in the program, folks. Unfortunately, Harper Larsen is unable to be here tonight, so I'll play the next song solo. Thanks for your understanding."

Harper frowned and looked at Maggie.

"Go ahead, honey," she said softly.

Applause erupted from the audience as Harper took the stage, her head held high. She gave Kane a tiny wave as she passed him and then sat at the piano facing him. He twisted around in his seat and locked eyes with Maggie standing in the wings.

A broad smile bloomed on his lips. "Thank you," he mouthed.

Maggie grinned at him in return.

"I stand corrected," he said into the mic. "Allow me to present Miss Harper Larsen performing a piano duel with me. This is "Magic Christmas Bells.""

Maggie's eyes welled as she watched Harper play with Kane. Joy was written all over the little girl's face. The song brought the house down. When they finished playing, Kane strode over to Harper, took her tiny hand in his, led her center stage and took their bows together—the striking handsome man in formal dress towering over the petite stunning girl. Her baby. Her man.

The standing ovation seemed to go on for minutes as Maggie clapped her hands raw and tears streamed down her face.

Mavis emerged from the other side of the stage toting a spray of red roses. She handed the flowers to Kane. He let go of Harper's hand and presented her with the bouquet, stooping to whisper in her ear. Harper smiled and nodded her head. She took her seat again at the piano and placed the roses on the bench next to her.

"Now is the time you have the chance to sing along with the chorus," Kane announced. "Harper is going to start us off."

He looked at the choir director and nodded. She faced the audience, raised her hands, and conducted the crowd in singing *Santa Claus is Coming to Town* to Harper's rousing accompaniment.

Kane hurried towards Maggie. But it seemed as if he moved in slow motion. Her breath caught in her throat and her heart pounded so strongly that she suspected he could hear her pulse. Kane embraced her—the most welcome completion and perfect fit in his arms. She wanted to remain safe in his arms forever, but he pulled away, cupped her face in his warm hands and kissed her softly—sweetly. The music and singing muted. Only Kane. Nothing else mattered.

"Thank you for coming back to me," he whispered, his mouth still inches from her lips, his dark eyes locked on hers. "We can work this out. I'll do whatever you want. Please say you'll come back to the house tonight and we can talk."

"I'll come back to your house tonight. I agree we need to talk."

"Good." He kissed her again. "Great. Come on."

Kane clasped her hand and towed her toward the stage.

She pulled back. "What are you doing?"

He towed her forward anyway. "I'm bringing you with me for the sing-along. There is no way I'll ever let you go again."

She laughed and proceeded out onto the brightly lit stage, hand in hand with Kane. Maggie took a seat on the piano bench next to him just as the choir started "Joy to the World."

Maggie looked at her radiant little girl across from her and then at the beaming man playing the piano beside her.

Unbridled joy burst inside Maggie. She knew in her heart that she and Harper were meant to be there with Kane.

Chapter 22

Mavis shepherded Maggie away from him, bound for a private room where she could change into her party dress. Kane ambled slowly towards the ballroom where the reception was in full swing while he went down a mental checklist. Maggie and Harper would come home with him that night! Was the house exactly the way he wanted to host them?

Harper's presents were still secreted in his closet. He had left all the rooms neat, and nothing was out of place. Kane's long habit of cleaning up after himself was second nature. The guest room bed linens were laundered, and the beds remade. He had washed the bath towels, too.

Wait. Maggie's ring is still on the kitchen counter.

He'd just steer them clear of the kitchen until he could regroup. Kane opened the heavy carved door and strode into the Christmas bedecked room. And then it hit him that he had left one of Harper's gifts out in the open. Kane glanced at his watch and calculated the required time to drive home, hide the present and come back to the reception.

Skye planted directly in his path interrupting his reverie. "I'm so happy for you, cuz!"

Kane smiled down at her. "Thanks. Aunt Kay said she'd come back."

"Mom's never wrong."

"Hey..." The thought occurred to him that Skye might help solve his predicament. "Would you mind helping me hide Harper's Christmas gift?"

"Which one..." She paused a beat until it dawned on her. "Oh... Sure. We need to leave anyway. The triplets are way past their bedtime. Leave it to me."

"You need the security code?"

"Duh, no. Even Scarlet, Serenity and Spring can remember 1234.

"Gabe, honey!" she called out, gaining her husband's attention. "Let's go get the terrors."

She bussed Kane's cheek and strode off holding Gabe's hand.

Kane drifted to the bar and snagged two flutes of champagne. As he turned away, glasses in hand, the door opened, and Maggie stepped into the room. She made eye contact with Kane and smiled at him as if his fondest dream had come true before his eyes. Wearing a dark green dress that clung to her figure in the most flattering ways, she had never looked so beautiful. And he had never felt more fortunate that she focused only on him.

Although he wanted her to enjoy the party and the cheerful community gathered for the celebration, Kane counted the minutes until he could suggest that they leave to have some time alone. He didn't have a solid plan for the rest of the evening other than somehow making sure he didn't do or say anything that would send Maggie fleeing again.

****

Kane handed her a glass of champagne and toasted, "To the most beautiful woman in the room."

The evening took on a dreamlike aspect for Maggie. She was amazed that her whirlwind trip from Chicago had ended as if perfectly orchestrated. Harper's virtuoso performance had her blown away, bursting with pride. Kane, tuxedo clad and gorgeous, had her starry-eyed and the desire evident in his smoky eyes had her weak-kneed. All the complications that needed sorting out receded amid glistening Christmas lights beneath his loving gaze.

A half hour into sipping champagne, nibbling on mini quiches, crab cakes and, her favorite tiny croissant-wrapped hot dogs, Maggie had trouble keeping her eyes open. She suspected that Harper was half asleep on her feet, also.

She touched Kane's sleeve. He cocked his head in response.

"I'm so tired. Do you mind if we call it a night?" she said into his ear.

Kane's eyes lit. "I thought you'd never ask."

He crooked his arm. She wrapped her fingers around his bicep, and he swept her out of the room. She collected Harper, who didn't voice the tiniest protest, from the solarium and they left the party exiting through the front doors, over the footbridge and into the small parking lot where Kane had parked his truck.

Maggie clicked her seatbelt in place and turned to Kane in the driver's seat. "My car is parked in the Wings store parking lot along Route 12. Gabe picked us up there. That's how we made it to the concert on time."

"I'll call the sheriff and explain. We can pick your car up tomorrow."

"Okay," she said and settled in for the ride.

Maggie dozed lightly during the forty-five-minute drive. The catnap left her refreshed when Kane parked in his driveway. Harper was deep asleep in the backseat.

"I've got her," Kane said softly.

He gently unfastened Harper's seatbelt and scooped her up into his arms. Maggie picked up her carry on, closed the backdoor of the truck and followed Kane, increasing her speed so she could beat him to his porch and open the front door ahead of him. She keyed in his security code as he swept past her carrying Harper down the hall toward the guest wing.

He gently lowered Harper onto the bed. "I'll go start a fire. Would you like a glass of wine?" he whispered.

"No thanks. Maybe a bottle of water?"

"You got it. I'll be in the family room."

She removed Harper's shoes and party dress, slipped a nightgown over her head, and then tucked the covers around her. The child didn't as much as flutter her eyelids. Maggie left the door a couple inches ajar and then went to find Kane.

He stood in his shirtsleeves in front of the blazing fire to the right of the lit Christmas tree. Flickers from the firelight and sparkles from the decorations cast a magical aura around him, blurring everything else in the room. Kane turned to face her and opened his arms. She slipped into his snug embrace closing her eyes, and he pressed her to his heart. She felt his pulse steady and strong as if his heart was beating with hers. One heart. One love.

"Oh Kane, I'm so sorry I ran off on you."

"Shush," he said. "There's nothing to apologize for."

Kane held her tighter, and she nestled her head against his shoulder marveling at how right it felt in his arms. Maggie opened her eyes and caught sight of a host of wrapped gifts under the Christmas tree.

"Look at all the presents." She took a step toward

the tree. "Oh my gosh." Maggie covered her mouth with her hand and turned toward him.

"What's the matter?"

"I completely forgot Harper's presents." Maggie wagged her head. "How could I forget?"

He hung his arm over her shoulder. "Santa won't disappoint Harper. Those gifts are all for her."

"They are? Wow. Why?"

"I have five Christmases to make up for."

His answer brought home the reality she had so far neglected to face. "Oh Kane." She sighed leaning her head against the side of his arm. "How in the world do we work this? She's too young. We can't tell Harper about sperm donation and surrogacy and biology and her aunt and uncle who would otherwise be her parents if they hadn't died."

"Of course not," he said softly. "But I've worked out a possible solution."

"You have? What is it?"

"Come with me to the kitchen and I'll show you."

"The kitchen? What..." She left the question hanging as he took hold of her hand and led her out of the room.

"My solution is over there on the counter." Kane dropped her hand, his eyes soft.

She gaped at the velvet box, unmistakably a ring box, perched on the marble counter. "Kane, is that...? Are you...?"

He strode over to the counter, picked up the box and stared down at it in his hand. He raised his eyes and gazed directly into Maggie's, riveting her to the spot.

"I love you, Maggie. Strangely, I feel like I've always loved you. Harper, too. All I know is that I want forever with you, Maggie. And I want more. I want a family with you. The family that I didn't know I started and the one, God willing, we make together. If you agree, Harper will have her daddy. I want bench love with you. Will you marry me?"

Tears sprang to her eyes. Maggie's heart raced wildly, and her hands started shaking. Her most far-flung dream come true stood in front of her with an open ring box in his hand and unmistakable love in his eyes.

"I love you so much, too, Kane. I say yes. Yes, to bench love."

Kane slipped the pretty ring on her finger and folded her in his arms.

****

Christmas morning dawned bringing Harper barging into Maggie's room. "Mommy, wake up. Santa came last night!"

"I'm awake, sweetie." Maggie rolled out of bed and slipped into the guest bathrobe hanging in the closet. She hadn't slept much that night leaving the bedside lamp turned on and outstretching her hand over and over to admire the sparkling emerald on her ring finger.

Despite her lack of sleep, Maggie was exhilarated. Her future with Kane stretched before her and she couldn't wait to become his wife.

She drifted into the den following the aroma of coffee and Christmas pine. Harper sat on her haunches beneath the tree thrumming with excitement.

Kane handed Maggie a mug of coffee and then sat down on the floor next to Harper. "Ready, set, go," he said.

Harper didn't have to be told twice. Kane handed gifts to his little girl one at a time. She unfastened bows and ripped off wrapping paper in a whirlwind of oohing and ahhing and thank you's.

Maggie's heart swelled watching them together.

He picked up a small gift box—the last under the tree. "This one isn't from Santa," he said. "It's from me."

Harper frowned and stared at the box. Kane could imagine what was running through her mind: how do you fit a daddy in a box?

"Trust me, Harper. This is the most special gift."

She tore off the paper and removed the box lid. Kane took out the delicate pendant necklace and dangled it in his hand in front of Harper. "Last night I asked your mommy to marry me, and she said yes. That means I'm going to be your daddy."

Harper let out a whoop. "My wish came true!"

He smiled and clasped the chain around her neck. She fingered the single pendant charm: a tiny glass bottle with a gold scroll inside engraved, I love you, topped with a red heart.

Maggie gaped at Kane. "Her wish?"

Kane nodded, yes. "I'll explain later."

"We have to go to the beach." Harper popped up off the floor. "I want to give you your bottle back."

"What does that mean?" Maggie said.

"Bear with me, sweetheart." Kane turned to Harper. "Let's go get some clothes on and we'll head to the beach."

Caught up in Harper's exuberance, and seemingly Kane's, too, Maggie changed into jeans and a top and met Kane and Harper out on the back deck. Kane sent a text and then he pocketed his phone and clasped Maggie's hand as Harper shot out onto the sand in the direction of the Inn of the Three Butterflies. The child raced ahead of them along the water's edge. In the distance Harper scooped something out of the ebbing tide, held it overhead and shouted, "I found it!"

Kane and Maggie reached Harper who presented Kane with a corked sea glass bottle etched with pelicans. "Here's your bottle," Harper said.

Maggie's jaw dropped. "Is that…?"

"Uh huh," he said. "Hey, Harper. Let's go stop by the inn. Miss Kay makes the best Christmas Day brunch."

She whizzed away from them.

He pulled a crumpled piece of paper out of his pocket and handed it to Maggie. "This is Harper's original wish. She rewrote it because of a misspelling, sealed it in this bottle and I threw it into the sea for her so she could make her Christmas wish in a bottle."

Maggie read the note. "I'm…speechless."

"Let's catch up with Harper," he said beaming at her and towing her into a jog.

When they reached their little girl Kane raised a hand overhead and waved in the direction of the inn. Maggie squinted in the sun and spied Skye coming down the deck stairs. She bent down and released a tiny yellow ball of fur.

The labrador puppy scampered directly to Harper who squealed in delight. She scooped the pup up into her arms and turned towards Maggie and Kane, giggling as the puppy licked the side of her neck, her eyes shining. "Oh, he's so cute!" she said.

Maggie petted the soft little body. "He's adorable. Kane, is this Skye's puppy?"

"No, he's Harper's."

"I can *keep* him?" Harper's eyes widened to saucers.

"Yep," Kane said. "Number 2 on your list."

"Oh boy! What should I name him?"

"Harper and Maggie, meet Tor."

"Tor? That's unusual," Maggie said.

Kane winked at her. "Short for Tornado."

Maggie covered her mouth and burst out laughing into her hand.

"Thank you *so* much," Harper sang out.

"Merry Christmas, Harper."

"Merry Christmas, Daddy."

A word about the author…

K.M. Daughters is the pen name for team writers and sisters, Pat Casiello and Kathie Clare. The pen name is dedicated to the memory of their parents, "K"ay and "M"ickey Lynch. K.M. Daughters is the author of 19 award winning, Amazon Best Selling, romance genre novels. The "Daughters" are wives, mothers and grandmothers residing in the Chicago suburbs and on the Outer Banks, North Carolina. Visitors are most welcome at http://www.kmdaughters.com.

Thank you for purchasing
this publication of The Wild Rose Press, Inc.

For questions or more information
contact us at
info@thewildrosepress.com.

The Wild Rose Press, Inc.
www.thewildrosepress.com

Milton Keynes UK
Ingram Content Group UK Ltd.
UKHW010233111224
452348UK00011B/736